DEADLY

PASSION

OTHER BOOKS BY AMANDA

Heaven's Heart Series
Deadly Passion
Benevolent Passion
Winged Passion
Ascending Passion

Immortal Vices and Virtues Series
Haunt Me

The Graced Series
Graced
Captive
Survivor
Bitten
Ashes
Freedom

The Moonlit Hills Series
Winter's Curse

HEAVEN'S HEART

DEADLY PASSION

BOOK ONE

AMANDA PILLAR

MAATKARE
BOOKS

Published by Maatkare Books
www.amandapillar.com

ISBN: 978-0-6480295-6-4

Cover Design: Amanda Pillar © 2021
Internal Layout: Amanda Pillar © 2018
Editor: Pete Kempshall

First Published August 2018

To Kel. Thanks for everything.

Chapter 1

Six Months Ago…

Shouts and screams emerged from the Inner Sanctum as people poured through the gold-veined marble hallways, their movements frantic. Azrael stood motionless, his silver-kissed wings held high off the ground as other angels surged past him on a wave of panic.

"It's gone!"

"We've been invaded!"

"Heaven is doomed!"

What is going on?

This chaos could not be supported. Not here, in one of the most holy areas of the Celestial City. Angels did not act like pathetic humans when confronted with discord.

Centuries of military training kicked in.

"Stop!" His shout thundered through the hall.

Silence descended, but for the sound of rustling feathers.

A youngster had tripped over close by, his blue robe hanging askew from a shoulder, pure white wings dragging on the ground. Shock was stamped indelibly on the boy's face. As Azrael helped him up, he met the lad's wild, pale green eyes with a stern gaze. "Tidy yourself up. And lift your wings."

Pink bloomed in the youth's cheeks as he obeyed.

Angelic faces taut with stress turned toward Azrael from every angle. He kept his posture relaxed, but hardened his expression so they could see his disdain for their behavior. "Return to your rooms in an orderly fashion. This is no place for strife."

One of the women stepped forward, her crystalline blue eyes awash with tears, her impossibly beautiful face smeared with soot. "But, Lord Azrael—"

Gentling his voice, he murmured, "I will go and see what has happened. You do not need to worry."

Surely it couldn't be as bad as these worshippers thought.

Cowed, the angels walked on past him at a more sedate pace, disappearing around a corner. But the tension hadn't left them, fear and anger marring their ethereally lovely expressions.

Azrael remained still, hands clasped before his belt, until the last glimpse of white wings had vanished. Not a thread of silver, gold or bronze had been visible in the plumage—every last angel had been a pilgrim.

He headed toward the Inner Sanctum, where two of his squadron, Dina and Zadkiel, had been stationed. Surely, if there had been such a breach, he would have heard from them—his unit had worked together for so long that they could generate mental connections with ease. Convinced the disturbance was nothing more than a minor infraction, he came to a sudden halt when he reached the large hall.

The room comprised an open chamber lined with soaring, cloud-colored columns, which drew the eye to a squat building in the middle of the expanse. It had the appearance of a human mausoleum, with delicate stonework and a recessed door.

Normally the hall was pristine. Now, the doorway to one of Heaven's most treasured artifacts had been destroyed, scorch marks scarring the walls. Tendrils of gray smoke swirled lazily through the air, and silver-flecked, ash-stained feathers wafted in the eddies, some splattered with crimson. The scent of blood, potent and iron-rich, hit him like a punch to the gut.

No.

Hurrying forward, he scanned the hall. Usually filled with a steady stream of worshippers, and guarded continually by members of his squadron, the Darts, it was now eerily devoid of people.

At the door to the sanctum, he paused. A gold bracelet lay on the ground, its delicate and expertly fashioned links broken; the small, rose-shaped diamond in its center glittered against the blood-and-feather speckled floor.

Dina.

As he squatted to pick up the piece of jewelry, he called out with his mind to the others in his squadron.

Come to the sanctum, now.

Three replied at once—Seraphina, Raziel and Yael.

Two didn't reply at all—Dina and Zadkiel.

Gripping the bracelet in his hand, he rose to his full height, turning to face the Inner Sanctum. He'd never seen inside before, despite the fact that he'd guarded the place for the last century. What lay within was one of their most valued artifacts, and could only be viewed by the worthiest of worthy, with access decreed by the archangels.

Heaven's Heart.

He sensed the others in his squadron approaching: fierce Seraphina, thoughtful Yael and intense Raziel, their second in-command.

"What happened?" Seraphina asked, her voice soft and lilting.

"I don't know." Azrael stepped into the forbidden chamber, and stared at the scorched walls, the bloodied floor and—

His heart slammed in his chest, his breath deserting his lungs in a rush.

The pedestal in the center of the chamber was bare.

It's gone.

No. *It couldn't be…*

For millennia, angels had guarded the Inner Sanctum. No one had ever breached the sacred walls, *no one*. The guards who'd been on duty had been two of the most formidable warriors angelkind had ever produced. And Dina…Dina was their captain, and so vicious a fighter even the archangels feared her in battle.

They'd been taken as well.

"What is it?" Raziel asked. His deep voice echoed in quiet.

Azrael spun on his heel, taking in the three remaining angels from his unit.

"Heaven's Heart has been taken."

❈

Archangels weren't known for their kindness. They ruled Heaven with an unyielding and often brutal hand.

Now that hand had come to rest on Azrael's shoulder.

Michael's words were quiet, but fury drenched every syllable. "You will *all* be punished for this."

Azrael knelt on the marble floor outside the Inner Sanctum, his gaze locked on the blood and burn marks that denoted where the door had been.

"Do you know who breached the walls?" Raziel asked. All four of them had been forced to their knees in front of their formerly impregnable sanctuary, to think about what they had done.

Which had been nothing.

Azrael didn't understand why they were *all* to be punished. Yes, he was a member of the squadron, but he had not been present during the attack. None of them had been. Dina and Zadkiel, who *had* been on guard duty, had clearly been overpowered, taken. What had happened to the rest of the angelic squadrons stationed throughout the city? Why were they not here as well?

Where was the blame being placed for Heaven being attacked in the first place?

The intruders had to have gotten in through a portal somewhere—the hall was only accessible on foot. You couldn't even enter on wings.

Michael's hand withdrew from Azrael's shoulder, but the feeling of menace remained. "At this stage, it does not matter who attacked us."

Azrael disagreed with that statement. Vehemently.

"Heaven's Heart has been stolen. Do you understand what you've all done?"

Since none of them knew what Heaven's Heart even

looked like, Azrael was certain no one could fathom what the theft meant.

"Sire," Raziel murmured, "if you will let us search, we will find the Heart and bring it back."

Michael strode into view. His long brown hair was tied back in a braid, and his eyes were pure white, with no iris or pupil. Massive wings soared over his shoulders, their gold threading a clear marker that he was an archangel. He had been one long before Azrael had been born, and would continue to be so probably long after he was dead.

"Oh, you will search for the Heart," he said. "But first, you must pay the price for your failure." A huge sword appeared in his right hand, the blade gleaming.

No.

Azrael fought to stand, but magic bound him in place, invisible ropes holding his limbs immobile. Soft footsteps sounded, and then another archangel came into view: Uriel, his ebony skin glinting with blue highlights. A susurration of feathers signaled more archangels had arrived, their power a pulse against Azrael's skin. The taste of fear was sour on his tongue.

"Word of this will have reached all of Heaven before sunset. Examples must be made."

"Examples?" Seraphina's voice held the slightest tremor.

Michael stepped closer. "You will all be exiled from Heaven. You will only be allowed to return if you find all three pieces of the Heart and give them to us."

Each word was like a blow to Azrael's chest.

"All *three* pieces?" Yael asked.

A short silence. "We guarded but one part of the

Heart," Michael said. "It is time all three were rejoined and stored here for safety."

Rage burned bright and hot within Azrael. The archangels were using them as scapegoats; setting them up for failure. He didn't doubt that Heaven had been searching for the other two pieces—if they even existed— for millennia. And now they were saying the only way for the Darts to return to Heaven was to find the elusive fragments.

"Can you give us any information on what we might seek?" Raziel asked.

Michael shook his head, his white eyes emotionless. "This is a punishment. We will not help you with it."

"Then we shall leave at once, so we may find the stolen piece and its brethren," Raziel said, taking charge.

But Uriel shook his head. "There is something else that must be done first."

Without warning, Azrael was shoved face-down onto the blood-stained marble floor. A strong hand grabbed one of his wings, holding it out straight, exposing the part where the tendons met the back muscles.

What are they doing—?

Agony roared through his body, setting every nerve ending alight. His vision hazed over. Another slice, and he was screaming, the pain so bad he'd thought he'd die. Prayed he would. He vomited, then collapsed, panting, as the others in his squadron shrieked in torment. The skin on his back grew slick, and dark specks danced in front of his eyes.

Then it was over.

The bonds that held him in place dissolved, but he couldn't move, his entire body throbbing from the brutal mutilation. Uriel's feet came into his line of vision, and the archangel dropped something in front of Azrael. Soft, feathery, with silver threads throughout. Bloody stumps where they had once joined living flesh.

Wings.

His wings.

CHAPTER 2

The Human Realm, Present Day

Drucilla didn't believe in fate, even though life seemed to enjoy screwing her over every other day. Unfortunately, today was no exception.

She placed her almost-empty glass of red wine on a polished mahogany table, which stretched down the side of the ballroom. Glittering crystal chandeliers hung from the center of the expansive space, while candelabras stood sentry on the edges. The air reeked of perfume, cologne and expensive alcohol.

Her target had been due to stop by about an hour ago, despite the party having started two hours prior. He believed in being fashionably late.

She scanned the wealthy attendees again. Most were well-dressed and coiffed demons who could pass as human—or don a human disguise—along with several high-powered homo sapiens. It was a mix of the highest echelons of New York society, people she had little time for, and who had no idea who she was. Or *what* she was, either. The demons had no clue, and as for the humans interspersed in the crowd...well, they were oblivious to any of the monsters lurking at their elbows. Literally.

"...so you can go home," her boss concluded.

She'd been ignoring him. It was a favorite pastime of hers.

"Wait." She replayed the half-heard conversation in her head. "What do you mean he's already dead?" she asked, wondering if she'd heard wrong.

Her boss—or, more accurately, her slave-master— gave her a crooked smile. Trick's tuxedo fit him like a second skin, and Dru noticed more than one woman eyeing him like he was a piece of delectable candy. He was handsome, she supposed, if you liked that whole golden-beauty-with-a-side-of-death kind of thing.

She didn't. Dru had never considered herself stupid. She hadn't become a slave because of something she'd done, rather because of something she *was*.

They were two totally different things, even if Trick didn't understand the nuance.

His smooth, bedroom voice pierced her thoughts. "A rival guild got to him early this afternoon."

She clenched her fist, her claws emerging with her anger. Pain burst to life in her palms, but she ignored it and the resulting trickle of blood. "Which one?"

Trick hadn't told her there was competition for her target. If she'd known, she'd have taken care of her rival first. Dru had never played well with others.

"The Falling Star," he said.

She frowned. They were a new outfit, having come to wider notice a mere six months ago. No one knew much about them, except that they were extremely efficient and, apparently, belonged to some scary-ass supernatural species.

And they'd just become number one on her personal hitlist. No one stole a job from her.

"Come now, Dru, don't look so annoyed." She plastered a fake smile on her face, and Trick's chocolatey-brown eyes narrowed. "I don't think that's much better."

"I don't like my plans being ruined."

He stroked her cheek in a proprietary manner, his expression almost tender. "So much anger."

She fought the urge to shrug off his hand. He might own her soul, but he had no claim on her body. Which, conversely, made him want her even more.

Trick didn't do well with denial.

He shook his head as he withdrew his hand. "Come now, it was just one job."

Just one job.

Right.

When you were a slave who had to earn your freedom, every job was significant, especially as Trick didn't particularly *want* her to end her association with the Halcyon Guild. He only gave her work when she threatened to destroy what little peace they had. She had become particularly good at manufacturing chaos. Dru liked to think it came with being half-human.

"I am going to go mingle," Trick said, stepping away. "Try not to kill anyone tonight. No one here is on any hitlist."

"*Yet.*" She flipped him off, got an answering smirk in return.

Despite having her own list of deserving candidates, Dru mostly killed for money—which in turn equated to her freedom. She tended not to murder people for being assholes; there'd be nobody left on the planet if she did that.

Aside from Peony.

Yeah, well, her sister was about the only person she knew who didn't annoy the Hell out of her. Not that they got along all that well—what with Dru being the reason Peony was also enslaved to Trick—but her sister was decent enough for someone who'd wanted to be a doctor.

Dru's eyes swept the crowd again, stopping at a mezzanine balcony that overhung the ballroom. Four figures stood there, three of them kitted out in evening wear that seemed molded to their physiques. Two wore tuxedoes, while the sole woman was adorned in a gorgeous floor-length designer gown. The last member of the group wore jeans and a T-shirt, totally out of place in the fancy mansion.

She knew at a glance that the four of them were a team. It was in their body language, the way they were all quarter-turned toward one another as they watched the party-goers below.

There was something about them, the way they moved maybe, that screamed military training.

Who are they?

She hadn't really paid too much attention to the invite Trick had gained her for the evening; she was only at the party because she'd known her target was attending. Or should have been.

Why is one of them in casual dress?

Alarm bells rang in her hindbrain. Something wasn't right with this shindig. And something was *really* not right with the four people on the balcony. Their faces, illumined by the light from the chandeliers, were inhumanly beautiful. More so than the standard succubus or incubus, who were generally hot enough to cause riots. But none of the partiers seemed to notice that they were up there.

Weird.

The man in the T-shirt swept his eyes over the ballroom once again, his gaze coming to a jarring stop as he met her stare. Shock bloomed over his gleaming caramel skin—he radiated power and sex. Then he turned away from the balcony and disappeared from view.

Shit. Was his surprise because he recognized her? No. She had the feeling it was something else…like no one was meant to be able to *see* him.

Time to leave.

Her quarry wasn't here and, well, there was no other reason she needed to stick around besides the fancy wine and tasty hors d'oeuvres that probably cost more than the last job she'd done. Turning toward one of the exits, she determined the quickest route to the front door then shoved her way through the throng, irritated at the way her dress hampered her movements. This was the last time she'd wear anything this body-hugging, that was for sure. She hadn't been able to conceal more than two knives, either.

Dru made her way to the hallway through the copious use of her elbows, which earned her numerous scowls and curses. She hoped none of the cursers were witches, or she'd soon be coming down with a bad case of pubic lice or something worse.

Nasty, inventive women, those witches.

She was almost at the door when a big hand squeezed her ass. Dru spun around to glare at the groper. The dude was tall, with such broad shoulders that he made a linebacker look puny.

Demon.

It was hard to tell what species he was, since he appeared human, but he could be any number of things. Some demons were as harmless as your pet gerbil; others were more dangerous than, well, her. But one thing was true about all demons, no matter the type.

Never back down.

No matter the species.

It might get you dead, but sometimes death was preferable to whatever they might do to you. She stepped forward and gave the demon a sugary smile, before cupping his balls in a firm grip.

His gravelly voice had a vaguely South African accent. "Hey sexy, you're a quick mover." He waggled an eyebrow. "I like that."

She moved closer, until her chest was almost touching him. Man, the guy was tall. She tightened her grip and he gave a strangled cry of pain; she'd let her claws prick his sack, but kept her toxin in check. "Don't ever touch me without permission, or the next time I grab your balls, it will be to shove them down your throat."

The demon paled and she let go; he backed up a few hurried steps, then quickly turned back to the group he'd been talking to previously, like nothing had happened. Hell, maybe he was used to that kind of rejection. His friends tried to look at her without making it obvious, so she gave them a cheerful wave. Fuckers.

He was lucky she'd held back, otherwise he'd be a

writhing, screaming mess. And he would have died, painfully. But Trick had told her to behave, and she just wanted to get out of there before that T-shirt clad demon—or whatever he was—found her.

Hurrying out into the foyer, she came to a sudden stop.

T-shirt guy was standing in her path. His arms were crossed over a broad chest that rippled with muscles just begging to be caressed. Challenge glinted in his pure blue eyes, and the aura of magic that clung to him made her grit her teeth. She had no idea what he was, but he was *powerful*.

He spoke, and her attention went to his mouth. It was kissable, suckable. If she didn't have a no-touching rule, she might even have considered making out with him a little, just to see if his lips were as sensual as they appeared.

But those distracting sexy-time thoughts were shattered when his words finally registered.

"Going somewhere?"

CHAPTER 3

Azrael hadn't intended to attend the event tonight, hosted by the remaining members of the Darts. He'd just finished his latest job and had wanted nothing more than to soak his body in a scalding hot shower. The scent of death clung to his skin in the mortal world, unlike when he'd been a warrior for Heaven. But the others had wanted to know how the hit had gone, and he'd figured he could clean himself up later.

He hadn't had much to report. The Sparta demon had been like all the others he'd ever seen—red-skinned, deceptively attractive, and greedy as the three circles of Hell. But that was demons for you. They all had foibles, and they were generally inappropriately good-looking. Oh, there were ugly ones, but most demons existed to tempt humans, and humans were very susceptible to a pretty face.

Unfortunately, contrary to the rumor that had led to Azrael taking this particular hit, the demon had had zero information about Heaven's Heart, or how to find it. He hadn't even known anything about Odin's Orb, another mystical item that the Darts thought would help find the three-part artifact.

Six months post-wingectomy, and he still wasn't any closer to understanding what Heaven's Heart actually *was*. And none of his former angelic colleagues were going to spill the beans, either. Hundreds of years of dedicated service, and he'd been thrown away like trash. The archangels hadn't even bothered to send a rescue party for Zadkiel or Dina. His two comrades could be rotting in the deepest, darkest corner of one of the Hells, and those gold-winged fools didn't care.

Rage turned his vision red, but he forced the emotion down with a deep breath. Anger was of no use, and he had another issue at hand. Specifically, the woman in front of him. He crossed his arms over his chest.

"Going somewhere?" he asked, deliberately blocking her path.

They were standing in a wide foyer decorated with centuries of accumulated wealth. The double doors were open and led out to a columned patio, where a Devilsgate waited to transport guests. People moved in and out of his peripheral vision: the well-dressed interspersed with the uniformed. The other Darts had stayed upstairs.

The woman's pale gray eyes narrowed, then she smiled and flicked a handful of nearly-white hair over her shoulder. It looked soft, like silk, and his fingers itched to touch the slippery strands. He'd never seen a human—or angel—with hair that exact color before.

"Just getting some fresh air," she said. There was a challenge in her eyes, like she was daring him to call her on her lie. Because she *was* lying, there was no doubt about that. Even though Azrael was a fallen angel, he still had some abilities: an inbuilt lie detector was one of them.

Plus, after she'd met his gaze a few minutes earlier, she'd high-tailed it out of the ballroom like her dress was on fire. Regular people—people with nothing to hide—didn't do that kind of thing. Then again, a regular person wouldn't have been able to *see* him or the others on that balcony, not through the spells of concealment that Raze had in place.

His eyes roved over her body, taking in her sleekly muscled figure and the skintight dress that meant she could have few concealed weapons on her person—if any. She was gorgeous, there was no doubt about that. Long-legged and with a face that would stop men in the street. But her body language and her expression spoke of slit throats and hidden bodies.

Was it wrong that he found the latter more attractive?

You've changed.

Yeah, well, getting your wings removed by force tended to do that. Whatever good had been in him had been excised that day, too.

"Let's get some fresh air together, then." Azrael gave her a small, practiced smile, the one he had come to understand melted the panties right off most women.

But she shook her head, her plump lips forming into a thin line. "I'm good."

Well, that's unusual.

He didn't think he'd ever been rejected by anyone before. Not when he'd been an angel, and certainly not since he'd fallen.

It wasn't that Azrael had an ego—facts were facts, after all. He was a fallen angel, and humans *loved* the fallen, as did a lot of demons. There was something irresistible about damaged goods, and an angel who'd lost his wings was certainly damaged. Plus, he was hot; he'd been told so countless times, *and* he owned a mirror.

"I insist. And since it's my party…" He let the sentence trail off and upped the wattage of his grin, holding out his arm in a gallant gesture.

She stared at the limb like it was diseased. "Fine."

But she didn't touch him.

Repressing a real smile, he indicated she should walk in front of him. She shook her head, strands of white hair slipping over her shoulder to cup one of her breasts.

He never thought he'd be jealous of hair.

She pointed at her face. "Eyes up."

He met her stare. "But the view is so nice."

A snort escaped her lush lips. He liked it, the surprised amusement real.

"You're a piece of work," she said. "Now, that fresh air you insist on?"

He didn't like her walking at his back, but she didn't seem to want him walking behind her, either. They fell into step beside each other as he headed down a hallway and toward the library. She was a tall woman—Azrael was well over six feet, but she came up to his chin. He wouldn't have to bend down much at all if they were to kiss…

You're an idiot.

Yeah, well. It seemed like the removal of his wings had activated another part of his anatomy…with a vengeance. Before, he'd been focused on his work, his purpose, and not much else. Sexual cravings hadn't really been part of his existence. Oh, he knew that other angels had those urgings, but he'd been largely ascetic, except for the occasional experiment.

Now, now he reveled in the feel of feminine flesh under his hands, loved sheathing his aching cock in their bodies. It was like a switch had been flipped on; why bother fighting it? What was the point? Even if he made it back to Heaven, he wasn't going to be the same angel as the one who'd died that day in the Inner Sanctum.

"You wanted to get some 'air' together, yet now you're as silent as a tomb." Her voice was dry, husky.

He could listen to her talk all day. Or more accurately, all night. While they were in bed together.

She'd kill you sooner than fuck you.

He liked a challenge.

"I didn't realize you wanted small talk," he replied.

She rolled her eyes. "Why else would you ask me to get some fresh air?"

They entered the dark, wood-paneled library. The scent of the books hit him—paper, dust, and knowledge. There wasn't much he loved about the Human Realm, but he did enjoy this place. Being surrounded by wisdom reminded him of home.

The scent of jasmine reached him as he edged past her to shut the door. A surprisingly innocent smell, considering her prickly nature. "There are plenty of reasons for 'fresh air'."

"We're in a library. Where's the freshness?"

"We aren't surrounded by people anymore?" He hadn't meant that to be a question.

She ignored his quip, instead studying the room with lethal intent.

Reminded of her earlier annoyance, he pointed at his face. "My eyes are here."

A wicked glance. "I'm just admiring all your...books."

Yeah, probably assessing all the egress points in the room. While her clingy black cocktail dress suggested otherwise, her entire persona read 'deadly'. Although, since she was human, he was safe—he was too powerful to fall victim to someone so frail.

"What's your name?" he asked.

A shuttered glance. "None of your business."

"Cute. My name is Azrael." He figured it wouldn't do any harm for her to have his real name. He wasn't living a top-secret existence, anyway. Neither were the others. After arriving on earth, they'd quickly formed the Falling Star mercenary company and proceeded to make a *lot* of money. It didn't hurt that Raze seemed to have been investing in the stock market since the thing had come into existence.

Funny what you learned about your squadron mates when duty and dogma were no longer in the way. Turned out Raze had been keeping lots of secrets, but that was fine with Azrael. They all had stories better left untold.

"Azrael? That's a bit...angelic, isn't it?" Despite the color of her hair, she had almost black eyebrows. One was raised in skepticism.

"My parents were ambitious." Perhaps he should have changed his name; angels *did* tend to inspire fear. But he wasn't interesting in hiding, he told himself.

"Right. Az it is."

He choked. Just a little. "*Az*?"

"Eh, less of a mouthful."

He winked, despite the disrespect to his name. "Oh, I can give you a real mouthful."

Her gaze dropped to his crotch. "I doubt that."

Burned.

Witty. He liked it. Skies, he liked *her*. Challenging, beautiful, and snarky. He could easily picture himself naked and tangled up with her, but that wasn't the reason he'd wanted her to come with him. Well, not the main reason, anyway.

He wouldn't say no to anything *should* it happen, though.

She crossed her arms, pushing up her ample breasts. He kept his focus on her face, barely. "Why did you need to bring me here? We could have just gone out the front door earlier, there was plenty of 'fresh air' there."

She had him there.

"What's your name?" he asked again, taking a step closer to her. He wondered what her lips would taste like. How soft her skin would feel.

"Call me Candy."

He knew that wasn't her real name, but he didn't care. At least he now had something he could shout later on, if everything went well.

He smirked. "I just have a couple of quick questions."

"I'm your captive audience, after all."

"How did you see me?"

"See you? You're standing right here." She waved at him.

"Before, when I was on the balcony."

She looked over his shoulder, avoiding eye contact. "I didn't see you."

"You looked right at me."

"There was no balcony."

She was saying the right thing, but she wasn't telling the truth. Again. "You're lying."

"No, I'm not."

He stepped closer still, until you couldn't slip a hand between them. "Yes, you are."

Her eyes flashed. "I didn't see anything. Now let me leave."

Everything about her was a challenge.

He leaned down, his lips touching hers in an almost-kiss. "Make me."

She moved in, pressing her mouth a little harder against his. "Since you said so."

Mmmm. She tasted sweet, like marshmallows. He swept his tongue out, to taste her further…but a burning pain scorched across his chest. He looked down and saw four slices ripped into his T-shirt. She'd drawn blood.

Great. This was one of his favorite tops.

He stumbled back a step, suddenly dizzy. "What—?" Pain spread through his nervous system like wildfire—it was as if acid had been poured into the wounds, flames raging through his veins.

She pushed him away, the palm of her hand against one of his pectorals, until the backs of his knees hit an armchair. He collapsed into the usually-comfortable leather, his legs giving out.

A hard tap on his cheek drew his attention away from the searing agony.

"It's going to hurt. A lot. Then you'll die. Sorry, but I have a strict no-touching rule. You just broke it. Ciao ciao!"

Truth, his brain shouted. Everything she'd said was truth.

Then she was gone.

CHAPTER 4

Dru closed the library door quietly behind her. Taking a deep breath, she held it in her lungs before slowly exhaling. She had no idea what that guy was, but he wasn't human or demon. Well, not a regular demon, anyway. And she'd just left him for dead in his own library.

Clever.

More like completely stupid. With a name that sounded a bit angelic, he probably wasn't anyone worth crossing. And she'd just killed him.

Time to get out of here.

No shit.

Turning to go, she almost bumped into a gorgeous woman with mahogany skin and eyes the color of milk chocolate. Her sleek golden dress was couture, her shoes and necklace both designer. *She'd been up on the balcony with Az.*

Great. Probably his buddy, come to check on him.

Dru made a show of smoothing down her dress and sweeping her pale hair behind her neck. She was suddenly grateful for the sheen on her lips. "You might want to give him a few minutes."

The woman's eyes searched Dru's, as if she could see inside her, to all the bad things that had been shoved into the furthest corner of her mind. Something in the primordial part of Dru's brain kicked in.

Don't lie to her.

This woman would be able to sense the deceit, Dru just *knew* it. And she didn't need to get detained here. Not now, not with Az dying on the other side of the door.

"A few minutes?" Her voice was like rough silk, slithering over Dru's skin.

Goddamn. She should bottle that.

But that voice meant this was no ordinary demon. She was powerful; Dru needed to get as far away from her as possible, before she discovered the dead body in the library.

"We got a little...busy...in there." She tried to look embarrassed.

The woman frowned, pursing her lips. "I see."

"I just need to get back to the party. I don't want anyone to know about this. I have a bit of a reputation."

All true, although her reputation was for avoiding the kind of scene she'd just painted for the woman.

That gaze again, but this time it was dismissive not probing, as if Dru had fallen beneath the woman's notice. "Of course."

Without waiting to see if the woman entered the library, Dru made a beeline for the front doors. She didn't stop, not even when Trick called after her. She just kept going, right out onto the gravel driveway, across the slightly damp manicured lawn, and up to the Devilsgate.

It had been in place for the guests all evening, and because it was purpose-made, it could take you to wherever you wanted to go.

Which suited her perfectly.

Stepping up to the gate, Dru quickly scanned her surroundings. No rushing bodyguards or angry beings. No lingering demons. Just Trick, outlined in the doorway, looking like he had some kind of freaking halo, and a beautiful formal garden that sprawled either side of the building.

"Halcyon Guild building, Tartarus," Dru muttered into the gate as quietly as she could. She wasn't sure if she needed to give the exact circle of Hell where the guild was established, but she wasn't going to go take a chance. She didn't want to end up in Sheol or Inferno.

The familiar tingle of magic spread over her skin as she stepped into the gate, and then she was gone.

Dru stumbled to a halt as she appeared in her room. It was one of the biggest rooms in the guild building, courtesy of Trick wanting to get into her pants. Not that he ever would, but the man lived in hope.

As far as Dru was concerned, you didn't shit where you ate, which meant that having sex with Trick was a bad, bad idea. Even if you didn't take her little genetic quirks into account.

Why could she still taste Az on her lips?

Just because he might have been the hottest man she'd ever seen, and he had a mouth made for sinning…

He's dead now, so get over it.

"Dru!"

Her twin sister, Peony, stood in the middle of the chamber, her face tired and worn. She wore hospital scrubs, despite not having set foot in a human medical facility since she had been enslaved to the Halcyon Guild a decade earlier.

Peony and Dru were identical at first glance—the same pale hair, the warm honey skin and the height—but no one had ever mistaken them for the same person. Dru liked to think the subtle differences in their appearances had formed because they hadn't met until they were adults; they had grown into their own identities and it had left an indelible stamp on their faces. Peony was soft, breakable, whereas Dru was hardened steel.

That's not fair. Just because she has a conscience and you don't...

Yeah, well. Being sold into slavery as a baby tended to erase any good a person might have had. Especially when you were enslaved to an assassin-training guild.

Her sister had been a healer—had even studied medicine at a human university—right up until Dru had entered her life and screwed everything up.

It's not all your fault.

No, Peony was a big girl, and she'd made her choices, too. But if it hadn't been for Dru tracking her down, her sister might have remained oblivious to the lower echelons of the world.

Peony wrung fine-boned hands together. "Dru, you're back!"

Dru strode further into the room and sat on the edge of her bed. She kicked off her high heels, sighing with instant relief. Damned impractical shoes. She wriggled her toes. "What's wrong?"

Peony bit her lip. "I don't like my latest assignment."

Yeah, well, Trick didn't exactly hand out the jobs based on enjoyment level.

"Peony—"

"No, it's not that I'm too soft." She slashed a trembling hand through the air. "Dru, this is dangerous. And *wrong*."

Dru frowned. Now that she thought about it, Peony didn't tend to get too worked up over her assignments. She generally just took whatever Trick gave her on the chin. Like Dru, she never got sent for the 'honey pot' jobs, because she was more likely to kill the target before they even got to the pillow-talk bit.

Being a full Mortus demon must suck.

Her sister was staring at her.

"All right," Dru said. "Why is it wrong?"

Peony glanced wildly about the room, as if checking for spies. Oh, there were listening devices here—Trick trusted no one—but Dru had already disabled them and placed spells over them, so he wouldn't notice they were broken. He'd hear Dru and Peony talking, but it would just sound like a regular argument.

They didn't have a great track record for calm discussions.

"Peony?"

Peony stepped forward, until she close enough to Dru that the scent of cinnamon and sugar was overwhelming. How her sister always carried the scent of baking, Dru had no idea.

"He has an angel here," Peony whispered.

"*What*?" Dru shoved to her feet so fast she knocked

Peony over.

Her sister sprawled on the floor, strands of pale hair covering half her face, her gloved hands smoothing the strands away from her cheeks. "Thanks."

"Ooops." Dru reached out a hand and then hauled Peony to her feet, careful to grip her sleeve. "He has a...a...."

She couldn't even say the word.

People like her, they hoped to never meet an angel in the flesh. Because it meant that said flesh had a severely limited life expectancy. Angels killed demons. Mercilessly and frequently. And halfbreeds—or cambions—like herself? Well, they weren't meant to exist. And angels took the 'natural order' very seriously.

"It's not right," Peony said.

"No, it's not." Dru balled her hand into a fist. "It's too dangerous."

Her gentle healer of a sister wouldn't be able to stand against an angel. Then again... "How did Trick get an angel?"

Peony flinched. "He's sick."

"Trick? You got that right." Their boss was as sick as they came, but he needed a shrink for what ailed him, not a regular doctor.

"Not Trick. The angel."

Angels got sick?

"I'm not following," Dru said. She was tired, and out of sorts, and she was starting to feel guilty. Maybe she shouldn't have slashed Az. "Start at the beginning."

"About a month ago, Trick showed me his new...recruit. The angel. And he was sick, like really sick. Poisoned with something, I don't know what. But it seems magical in origin, maybe demonic, I don't know. I've been looking after him as my latest 'assignment'." She made finger quotes around the last word.

When Peony sold her soul into slavery, she'd made a deal with Trick. She would work off the debt, like Dru, until the slate had been wiped clean. Except Peony was horrendous at being an assassin. She couldn't even stomp on a Hell roach, let along slit someone's throat. So Trick had had to find her tasks she could do; ones that wouldn't result in her puking, or getting herself killed. Thankfully, however, mercenaries tended to accrue a lot of injuries, which meant that Peony was kept busy.

But an angel…

"Is it dying?" Dru asked. A thought struck her. "Does it still have…*wings*?"

Peony winced. "Yes to the wings, and probably to the dying."

It has wings.

"Has it tried to attack you?"

Her sister shook her head, a strange emotion flittering through her expression. It was gone before Dru could work out what it was. "No. But he says his friends will come for him. And I believe him. They will kill whoever they can to get to him, that I don't doubt."

Raided by angels.

It would destroy the guild. Not just because angels were scary-ass bastards who killed demons on sight, but because the Halcyon Guild's reputation would be shattered if they were successfully attacked by damned do-gooders. No demon would work with them again.

"Those wings must be worth a fortune," Dru muttered. Angel feathers were highly prized in blood magic.

"No feathers are left. They're all but destroyed from whatever poison he was given."

Dru shut her eyes for a few seconds. At least Trick hadn't been selling angel feathers. That would have been painting a target on their back and then some. "So, what do you want me to do about it?"

"Help me?"

"This kind of job would be top secret. How am I going to approach Trick about it? It could mean you get hurt." 'Hurt' being an euphemism for 'dead'.

"You could find the angel on your own? Then say something about your discovery."

Dru eyed her sister. "And how easy would that be?"

"Not easy."

Despite their troubled relationship, she didn't want anything bad to happen to Peony. Her sister had a good heart, and she was the only blood relative that Dru had any contact with. If Dru had been raised in the Human Realm with Peony, they might have even been best friends. But life had had a different plan for them.

"I'll see what I can do without risking your life."

Peony reached out a gloved hand, letting it hover over Dru's shoulder. Her sister's mutation meant that she struggled to touch anyone without gloves, and her physical avoidance was ingrained. "Thank you."

But Dru shook her head. "Don't thank me yet."

Things had a tendency to go wrong, at least where she was concerned.

CHAPTER 5

The pain had taken hold of his entire body, agony spearing through him worse than anything but losing his wings. Hands forming into fists, Azrael tried to shout out mentally to the others, but a gray haze blocked his efforts.

What the Hell had she poisoned him with?

The door to the library opened quietly—almost tentatively—and for a moment, he thought that the devil-woman had returned to finish him off, or to help him.

Stupid.

Because it wasn't her.

Seraphina stood framed in the doorway, her long, dark hair woven into dozens of braids and piled high on her head. "Azrael!"

She shut the door and hurried into the library, stopping in front of him. Her training kicked in, and she moved away quickly to check the room for intruders—only then did she bend over him to examine the scratches on his chest. Blood still seeped from wounds that should have closed within seconds of being made.

"What happened?"

"Wrrrmm."

Had he said that?

From the concern that flashed across Seraphina's face, his guess was yes. He tried again, forcing words out of his tight throat. "Woman."

Seraphina's eyes flared. Then she frowned, her gaze becoming vacant for a moment before returning to sharp focus. "I've let the others know."

He wanted to nod, but it was all he could do to keep his head upright. She reached out to touch the wounds, but he gasped, "P-poison."

She drew back. "I'll be careful."

Cautiously, she took hold of his T-shirt's collar, then ripped the garment in half. The slashes had only just begun to crust over, and tearing away the material took the newly formed scabs with it, but the pain was negligible in comparison to the fire in his veins.

The wounds were beginning to heal.

Relief slammed through him, sharp and intense. He wasn't dying. Not if his body was already trying to mend the damage.

But—

"Pain." The word was gritted out.

"She must have injected some venom or a toxin into the wounds. But they are beginning to heal, and you aren't dead. You must be fighting it off, whatever it was."

No, he wasn't dead. Even though a few minutes earlier he might have wished he had been.

The pain is getting better.

He still couldn't bear to move his body, not even an inch, but the torment was mutating into waves of hurt, rather than the relentless surge that had threatened his sanity and took him back to writhing on the floor of the Inner Sanctum.

Raze burst in, Yael close on his heels. The three of them stood in a small semi-circle in front of Azrael's chair, Raze's expression taut with anger, but Yael's amused.

"Find...funny?" Azrael forced out.

"You're alive." Yael's hazel eyes glittered. "And you got done over by a small half-human woman. It is a *bit* funny."

"Yael—" Raze warned.

"What? He can try to beat me up for it later."

Well, he wasn't about to do anything now, and Yael knew it. The jerk. It was strange how you could spend centuries working with someone and never know they had a subversive—and annoying—sense of humor.

Raze sighed. "We couldn't find the woman. Apparently, she left through the gate shortly after your...run-in."

"It's my fault," Seraphina said, shame-faced. "I bumped into her outside the library, and she made it sound like you two had been...trysting. I thought to give you more time before coming in. When you never returned to us, I came to investigate."

Her words made a different type of fire rage through him. It wasn't her fault. It was his. He'd ignored the woman's demeanor and aura, and had assumed she was relatively harmless because she'd looked human.

His mistake.

No one else's.

"It's...okay." The words came out more easily. "No harm done."

Seraphina's eyes went wide.

"No lasting harm," he amended.

Well, he hoped that was the case. The woman could have infected him with some crazy demon-virus or something. He really shouldn't have kissed her, and the fact that the marshmallowy taste of her was still on his tongue only irritated him more.

"Azrael—" Seraphina began.

"It's fine." Now that the pain was receding, and he could feel the wounds closing, he was confused, irritated and, well, *embarrassed*. They'd all rushed here to find him laid low by a few claw marks.

No wonder Yael thought it was hilarious. Azrael probably would have laughed, too, if it had happened to one of the others.

He was just lucky that despite his lost wings, he still had the constitution of an angel. The benefit of being fallen, but not lost. Otherwise, he might have been worm food right about now. He'd ponder his good fortune in more detail later.

Enough.

His three companions were staring at him like he was a science experiment—or worse, something to be pitied, just a little. He wanted the subject changed, and quick.

"Seraphina, why were you looking for me?"

She shifted her stance slightly. "We have another lead on Odin's Orb."

"That last lead was a piece of shit." Azrael lifted his arm and ran a hand through his hair. The pain was bearable enough now for small movements.

"We couldn't have known that," Raze said. "We need to check out every lead. The Orb could help us find Dina or Zadkiel, or even the pieces of Heaven's Heart itself."

"It's a demon-powered artifact. You know the rules about those." Azrael didn't know why that bothered him so much, considering he'd taken up a career in assassination after his fall. Even he had his limits, apparently, and looking for Heaven's salvation in a demon-powered device was a little too ironic.

"They took our wings." Yael's expression turned flat. "They threw us out of Heaven, and they gave us no help. We can only use the tools available to us, and if they include demon devices, such is life."

"We have no choice. We can't use Heaven's artifacts," Seraphina added.

Well, he didn't have to like it. "There are only so many lines we can cross before they won't accept us back into Heaven, even if we do succeed."

He wasn't going to admit it to the others, but he didn't know if he even *wanted* back into Heaven anymore. The archangels had used and discarded them like trash. Did he really want to spend the rest of his immortal life working for those assholes?

So, do you really care if you find this demonic artifact?

It didn't matter to him, no. But for the others…Yes, he realized. He'd cross the line for them. He wanted them to have the chance to win back their wings and their former places in Heaven.

"We can't leave Dina and Zadkiel to rot," Raze said.

"No," Azrael agreed.

In the six months since their two comrades been taken, the fallen angels had used as many tracking spells as they could, but the missing pair weren't in the human or angelic realms. Which left Hell, and its three circles of pain, misery and horror: Tartarus, Sheol and Inferno.

Only the archangels had dealings with the rulers of the underworld, and even then, it was only to ensure humanity never learned of the supernatural world's existence. Beyond the religious texts, at any rate.

Azrael stretched his legs. The muscles screamed, cramped by the poison's onslaught. But this new discomfort was a good pain; his limbs were coming back under his control.

"You want me to go looking for the Orb?" he asked.

Raze took in Azrael's bloody chest. "One of us probably should…"

"I'm the one who has kept the lowest profile. People already know what you three look like." They'd used Raze's money and connections to secure the house and the first contracts; Seraphina's beauty was what had won them access to some of the more select areas of the underworld; and Yael…well, Azrael wasn't sure what he did exactly, but he'd been out in public more than Azrael to do it.

"I'm not as well-known as the other two," Yael said. "I can do it."

"You'll get your suit dirty," Azrael muttered.

"There's something to be said for a well-tailored suit."

He rolled his eyes. "Yeah, that the devil wears Prada or some shit."

"Enough with the bickering," Raze growled. He nodded at Azrael. "If you're well, you can go. Yael, we'll keep you as back-up, in case we get any other leads. You're better at hiding in plain sight anyway."

Yael didn't look too happy about it, but he nodded his assent.

"So, where is the Orb?" Azrael asked.

A knife-edged smile slashed across Raze's face. "In Inferno."

Of course, it is.

"Where in Inferno?" That circle of Hell was ruled by Satan, the original sinner, and he didn't really like angels, at least those who weren't lost. It'd be dangerous entering his territory alone. But for the others, Azrael would do it.

"A dark sorcerer by the name of Set has it. You'll have fun extracting it from him."

Great. Seth. Set. A former Egyptian god.

This was going to be a piece of cake.

Not.

CHAPTER 6

Dru walked with Peony back into the main hall of the guild, where she watched as her sister disappeared down one of the corridors. She was tempted to follow her, to see where this angel was being held, but right now was not the time.

"Dru!"

Trick was striding into the hall, his blond hair wind-mussed and his expression sterner than she'd ever seen before. Directed at her, anyway.

Trick smiled even when he killed people.

He came to a stop in front of her, his brown eyes glittering dangerously. "We need to talk. Now."

"Sure, boss."

He looked even less impressed with her response than normal. She followed him out the hall and down one of the main corridors. They stopped outside his office.

That isn't a good sign.

Trick generally did his business in the hall, so everyone knew what was going on. That, and so everyone could see what happened to those who displeased him. He rarely asked for one-on-one sessions.

"Well?" He stood holding the door open for her.

"Well, what?" She strode into the room, which was largely bare, except for an Ikea-style desk and a few bookshelves on which sat bits and pieces of…people.

"You were daydreaming." He took a seat behind his desk.

There were no chairs in front.

The little power-plays of the head-honcho. Which was fine, Dru could stand for hours, especially since she'd shed her high heels. She probably should have put some shoes on, though. Her feet were growing chilled.

"I don't daydream."

"Not even about handsome guys in black T-shirts?"

Her attention snapped to him. Was he jealous? "I don't remember any guys in black T-shirts," she lied.

"Oh? You don't? You didn't just disappear into a room with one earlier tonight?"

Fuck.

Maybe Trick *was* jealous.

She'd thought his fixation on her stemmed primarily from his desire to have sex with her, simply because he *couldn't*. What if—*gah*—he actually *liked* her or something?

Dru shoved some of hair back over her shoulder. "Him? He was nothing more than a blip on my radar."

Sure, he'd been the sexiest guy she'd ever seen, but he tried to kiss her, without her permission. And she didn't take kindly to that type of behavior. From anybody. It didn't matter that when she'd met him, she'd fantasized—just a little—about what it would be like to make out with him. Fantasy and reality were two totally different things.

She could have one, but not the other.

"Then why were his friends searching for you after?" Trick demanded. He leaned forward in his chair.

Her stomach sank. "They were?"

She inspected her nails, which still had some crusty bits of blood on them. *Gross.* She should have washed them, rather than focus on removing her shoes. "I *may* have killed him."

Trick exploded from his chair, the furniture slamming against the wall behind him, and the desk moving forward half a foot. "You *what*?"

"I said, 'I may have killed him'." She gave him a look that said *duh*.

Trick righted his chair and sat. "Dru, you're an idiot."

"What?" She crossed her arms over her chest.

"Didn't I specifically tell you not to kill anyone?"

"You said to *try* not to kill anyone." Her jaw clenched. Something was going on here, but she didn't know what. Her boss didn't normally care what she did in her free time, provided it didn't reflect badly on the guild.

This may reflect badly on the guild.

Fine. Maybe she *did* know what was going on.

"Why did you kill him?" Trick's expression was tired. "You're sure he's actually dead?"

Maybe she *had* been too hasty. "I clawed him up a bit."

Trick groaned.

For most demons, a small scratch wouldn't be a big deal, but her nails secreted a poison so virulent it could kill pretty much anything. The only creatures immune to it were other Mortus demons, or her potential 'mate'. Maybe angels too, but that was up for debate, according to everything she'd read.

There was a reason her species lived in a dark corner of Inferno. They were some of the nastiest demons out there, *and* they were directly descended from Satan himself. And while she hadn't confirmed Az was dead, like she would have if he'd been a regular hit, she had no doubt he was. Her poison was more virulent than even the most toxic Hell-beast.

Thanks, Grandpa Satan.

Dru somehow doubted the Hell-lord would appreciate being called that.

"Do you have any idea what that guy was?" Trick asked.

"No. But he seemed powerful."

"I think they're fallen angels."

Aww, Hells.

Az hadn't even tried to hide it—he'd told her his name and she'd thought it was angelic-sounding. She was a complete and utter fool.

"He got handsy." Dru hadn't meant to sound so defensive.

Trick studied her, the iciness in his brown eyes thawing a little. "You're going to have to lay low for a while. They have serious money, and if they *are* fallen, then they'll be powerful, as well. And probably nasty as Hell. Angels don't fall without a reason."

Trust her luck.

She considered asking Trick how he knew Az and his friends might be angels, but then he was in charge of the Halcyon Guild—he had access to plenty of info. "Got a job for me?" she asked instead. "I can go to ground while doing it. And it had better be a decent one, after you didn't tell me I had competition for the Sparta demon."

Trick grunted. "You just killed a fallen angel and you're trying to dictate to *me*?"

"I don't play well with others, you know that. He tried to touch what wasn't his. Not my fault." She tightened her jaw, forcing the rest of the words back inside. It wouldn't do to annoy her boss any more than she already had. And if he was jealous—

She certainly wasn't going to admit that for the *tiniest*, smallest instant she *might* have enjoyed Az's kiss…

Trick grabbed a scroll that had been next to his left arm. "A new hit came out today. From Hades."

Hades.

Wonderful.

Hades was the ruler of Tartarus and he wasn't known for his kindness or patience. He was widely regarded as a right bastard, the last of the Greek gods to have survived the Great Culling. Only a few other old deities remained, and Hades had kept his job through sheer strength and brutality. Oh, and by having one of the largest packs of Hellhounds within *all* of the Hells at his disposal. Rumor also persisted that he might even have a demi-god as his personal assistant, although no one had ever proven it. Or lived to tell, anyway.

"Why doesn't he just kill the target himself?" Dru asked.

"Because the target lives in Satan's territory. Name's Set."

Set.

Oh, come on.

Her day was just getting better and better. Not. But at least this meant she *had* to keep a low profile while on the job: no visiting other guilds, no meet-and-greets with Trick's buddies. Plus, Inferno wasn't a great place for assassins who didn't belong to that realm, not unless they were there as dinner guests. Commercial competition wasn't generally encouraged.

Still, the location explained why Hades had given the task to the guilds. He technically couldn't interfere in another Hell-lord's territory, although assassination was allowed.

However, her mind got tangled on one little detail. "The target is *Set*? Really?"

One of Trick's eyebrows rose. "You've heard of him?"

"He's a former Egyptian god. *Of course* I've heard of him."

Trick shot her a dubious look.

"What? I paid attention in school." Well, she'd paid attention to the limited schooling she'd gotten. Her trigonometry still sucked, but there wasn't much call for that skill in her line of work, so she didn't let it bother her. Much.

It was just hard sometimes, when she had a twin who had been university-educated. It showed her what she could have had—could have become—had she not been sold into slavery as a babe. "Set was the God of Chaos. Cut his brother up into tiny pieces and scattered him across the kingdom. Vindictive much?"

"Fine. You know who Set is. Then you know his fortress is *almost* impossible to penetrate."

"Did you really have to use the word 'penetrate'? I'm not sure it was warranted."

Trick glared at her. "I can give this job to someone else. In fact, I will."

He made to stand, palms pressed flat to his desk, muscles tensing.

"No, this is mine," she said. "I'm one of your best assassins, you know that."

"Yes, but you're a liability at the moment."

"Gee, thanks." She pursed her lips.

"Dru, I'm not even sure this mission can be done. I was thinking about rejecting it."

"And risk pissing off Hades?"

"I said I was 'thinking' about it. Not that I'd decided on it."

She was being manipulated, but she didn't care. She had to lay low for a while, and going after the near-impossible-to-defeat Set sounded like a decent way to do it. It'd keep her mind occupied, at any rate.

"I'll need some serious magical support," Dru said, thinking. Invisibility spells, magical grenades, flash-bombs…

"I'll see what I can arrange."

Trick would do right by her, she didn't doubt that. Plus, killing a former god would more than pay for whatever supplies she needed, their reputation would skyrocket, and they'd put those Falling Star pricks to shame.

"I'll go and start packing. Tell Hades we accept." As she turned to go, she realized she hadn't spoken to Trick about Peony. Dru really was a terrible sibling. *Before I go, I'll say something.* But there wasn't really any way she could work it into the conversation and have it appear natural. At least, that's what she told herself as she reached the door.

She was worried about Peony, but as long as her sister

kept her head down and didn't piss off Trick or the angel, she'd survive.

Surviving isn't living.

No, but it was the best you could hope for sometimes.

She'd say something when she got back. She *would.* It would give her more time to plan how to approach Trick, anyway.

Her boss' voice pulled her up short, just past the doorway. She stepped back inside the office, leaning on the door.

"Oh, and while you're at Set's fortress, there's something I want you to look for."

And here is the axe.

"What would that be?" she asked, worry zapping through her. This was probably the main reason Trick wanted the job. That, and not angering Hades.

"Set supposedly has an ancient artifact called Odin's Orb in his collection. I want you to try and find it. Once you make the kill, of course. That is, naturally, the priority."

He was stressing that the hit was the main gig a little too much. Which meant that he *really* wanted that Orb.

Wonderful. A magical artifact. Just what she *didn't* want to be handling. Those things had a habit of backfiring.

"Odin's Orb? Is there any description of it?" she asked.

Trick stared at her. "It's an *orb.*"

Yeah, *she* was the moron in this conversation.

"So? I look for a sphere. Great. There isn't going to be anything else like it at an ancient sorcerer's lair, is there?" She probably shouldn't have used quite that much sarcasm, since Trick was probably still annoyed with her, but whatever. She didn't like going into a situation unprepared, and this whole Orb-extraction screamed 'lack of planning'.

Trick frowned. "To be fair, there isn't much of a description about the Orb's physical appearance. Set killed Odin during the Great Culling, stole the Orb, and has kept it under lock and key ever since."

"Along with a million other treasures."

"I'll see what I can dig up on a physical description before you leave."

Dru gave him a sickly-sweet smile over her shoulder. "Thanks. You're a huge help."

"Don't be an asshole, Dru."

She shrugged. "I don't know how to be anything else."

CHAPTER 7

Peony hadn't lied to her sister.

This assignment really was a terrible idea on Trick's part. She might have grown up in the Human Realm, but even she knew that keeping an angel chained up in the basement was a bad plan. As if the angel would ever want to serve them, even if it had been sold into blood slavery.

Peony paused outside the door and ran trembling hands over her scrubs, then tugged on some gloves from the supply cart next to her. She could never be too careful—she'd learned the hard way that being half-Mortus demon was deadly to pretty much everyone.

Even the mother who'd raised her.

Breathe deep. Bury the memories, focus on the now.

There. She was ready.

Unlocking the cell, Peony stepped into the stone-walled prison, her eyes instantly homing in on the emaciated figure on the floor. She kept putting him on the bed, he kept throwing himself onto the straw-covered ground. It was a silent battle of theirs, but she persisted.

Nobody should have to sleep on the floor. Especially

not in a cell.

She dragged the medical cart inside, then checked the door had locked behind her. She didn't know why, but this man unsettled her like no other. Maybe it was because, despite his physical state, his gaze was so piercing it hurt.

It was like he saw inside her, to the very core of her being. And was surprised by what he found.

She moved closer and discovered that he was asleep— at least, his eyes were closed. His scalp had been shaved recently, but tiny sprinkles of blond hair had started to grow back in the time she'd been looking after him. His pale skin looked like it hadn't seen the sun in an age, and he was covered in mottled bruises from whatever poison was attacking him.

But he was getting better.

His eyelids fluttered open, and emerald green eyes locked with hers. "It's that time already?" His voice was low and musical, and it made her skin tingle in a way she preferred not to think about.

"Will you help me lift you up?" Peony asked.

A grunt was her reply.

Careful of his shredded wings, she hooked her arms under the angel's torso and lifted him onto the stone bed. He didn't make a sound while she did it, even though she knew it must have hurt him. She broke the contact, wondering how he still managed to smell so nice, even though he hadn't bathed in a while.

Must be an angel thing.

New bruises bled under his skin from where she touched him. She bit her lip at the sight.

"They're fine." His gaze bore into her. "The bruises.

Don't worry about them."

"I'm your doctor, I have to worry about them."

"And whoever heard of a demon doctor before?" He shook his head slightly.

He often said things like that, as if he was surprised each time she came to treat him. She figured that when you were an angel, good and evil were pretty straightforward: Heaven was host to the good guys, and Hell was host to the bad ones. But she'd come to understand that there were many shades of gray in the world, and her life had been very much lacking in stark whites and deep blacks.

"I've been tending to you for weeks; I'm not going anywhere until you're well." As if she could leave, anyway. She'd sold herself into blood slavery for two centuries, and she'd only served ten years of her contract.

"How did an angel get sold into demon slavery, anyway?" Peony almost slapped a hand over her mouth. She hadn't meant to say that out loud. Sure, she'd wondered it over and over, but to ask the question…That was cruel, and she wasn't like that.

Plus, she'd been there when his sellers had brought him to Trick. She knew it hadn't been voluntary.

He snorted, something like bitter amusement dancing across his emaciated features. "We weren't prepared and we got raided. I was taken. My friends will come get me. I've told you that."

"You told me the latter." She shrugged, trying to act casual and like she hadn't just been an asshole. But…she couldn't encourage him in his delusion. "Everyone can have daydreams, I guess. But just remember, they're dreams. You're deep in Hell now." She placed the blood-pressure cuff on his arm, wincing at the bruises that formed when she inflated it.

Having his friends come for him would be horrible for the guild, for Dru, and for her. Despite what anyone might think, Peony really, *really*, wanted to live. She didn't want her new home raided by angels, and since she'd been the one to spend the most time with the angel, she'd probably be the first to die. If they managed to get in. And as far as she was concerned, that was a big *if*.

"What are your daydreams?" The soft question intruded on her thoughts.

Peony paused while taking his blood pressure. "I don't have any. Not anymore. There's no point."

She'd firmly shut the door on her goals the day she'd signed on the dotted line with Trick. It was impossible to work as a doctor when your soul was enslaved to a demanding master. And well, she'd never really had the white-picket-fence kind of dreams that other girls did. Hard to believe you could ever have a family when your touch equated to death.

"I thought demons always wanted what they can't have," the angel murmured.

"And I thought angels were smarmy jerks who thought they were better than everyone else." Damn it. Asshole behavior again.

But he huffed out a laugh. "Touché."

He'd been beautiful, she realized. The mirth had briefly hidden the pain and discomfort that usually marked his face and, with his green eyes sparkling, Peony realized he'd been stunning.

Of course he was. He's an angel.

Yeah, well, his looks didn't matter. She was more

interested on what was happening *inside* him. This was the chattiest he'd ever been, and she took it as a sign that he was feeling better, even though he didn't show it. Physical changes could be happening on the molecular level that she couldn't see.

She put the stethoscope down and ripped the Velcro open on the cuff. One-twenty over eighty. She wasn't sure what normal blood pressure was for an angel, but that was good for a human. As she rummaged around the cart for a set of baby wipes, she asked, "What's your name?"

He turned his attention to the wall. "I don't have one anymore."

"Why not?"

"When I was taken, I lost my right to my wings."

She frowned. "Is that why they're…dying?"

"No."

But he didn't elaborate. It made treating him all the more difficult. Fighting back a frustrated growl, she finished her daily observations, then cleaned him up as best she could with wet wipes. "You'll live for another day."

Of that, she was certain. Of what plagued him, she had no idea. It was a poison of some kind, one that his body was neutralizing, but very slowly.

She cleaned up her equipment, then pushed the cart toward the door.

He called out, his lyrical voice halting. "Was there…another angel brought here with me?" He'd half-raised himself up on an elbow.

"Another *angel*?"

A slight nod.

"No."

There were two *of them?*

Trick had only been able to get his hands on one of them, because she hadn't been asked to look at any other winged creatures.

So many questions, and she was *really* better off not knowing the answers to any of them.

The angel lay back down, but as Peony opened the door, she heard him mutter, "Z."

"What?" She looked over her shoulder at him.

"Call me Z."

CHAPTER 8

Inferno wasn't anything like he'd expected.

Hell was meant to be a barren wasteland full of raging lava pits and disgusting monsters. And while he suspected that there were plenty of areas in Hell that lived up to that reputation, the area surrounding Set's fortress was the exact opposite. Lush green rolling hills, orchards filled with ripe fruit, a winding river, and a lovely blue sky overhead—some might have mistaken it for Heaven.

Maybe Satan had a sense of humor.

Either way, Azrael was on guard. He wasn't up to full strength, courtesy of 'Candy's' venom, but didn't have time to waste. A contract had been placed on Set's head, and he couldn't let the competition get to the former deity before he did.

That Orb was his.

No matter that Azrael doubted its power, that he doubted it would lead them to the pieces of Heaven's Heart—the others wanted it, and he wasn't about to let them down. Not after the fiasco from the previous night.

Yael had laughed him out the door this morning. Jerk.

Lurking next to a stone arch that marked the edge of Set's territory, he took in the fortress that protruded obscenely from the fertile surroundings. It had rough black stone walls at least fifteen feet high, tipped in shards of razor-sharp glass. The glimmering light of spells was also visible on the stone's surface — and he had no way of knowing what they'd do. Oh, he could read some of the symbols, but Set had mixed in demonic languages with his native hieroglyphs, plus a few other phrases Azrael hadn't seen before.

He guessed he'd find out when he got to them.

The benefit of being an angel in Hell, though, was that most of those spells would likely be keyed to demonic lifeforces. There were very few angels who'd step foot this deep into Hell to go after a former god, and Set probably assumed he was safe from their attack.

He sliced the skin on his forearm and exhaled with a hiss, the pain brief and sharp. Then he dabbed a finger in the welling blood and drew the angelic glyph for invisibility on the center of his chest, before dropping his shirt back into place. A heartbeat later, and he couldn't even see himself. The spell would only last two hours, thanks to his reduced strength, but hopefully it was enough time to get him inside the fortress and close enough to Set to not have to worry about being caught on the way in.

He jogged straight along the road to the fortress' entrance. The large metal gates were down, but that didn't matter. He could climb. After making sure his backpack and gear were on securely, he paused to study the walls. There were plenty of hand-holds he could use.

As he gripped the wall, a surge of dark magic shot through him with an electric zap. He clenched his teeth against the discomfort. *Damn.* That was stronger than he'd anticipated. Maybe deposed gods still packed a punch. Considering Set had managed to survive the Great Culling, Azrael had been a fool to think otherwise.

Reaching above his head, he began to pull himself up the wall, each movement causing a new bolt of electricity to shoot through him. He dodged the shimmering edges of any spells he could see, hoping to avoid accidentally triggering them through sheer proximity. Then he was at the top, his face level with those nasty pieces of glass. He studied the shards: their surfaces were smeared and sticky.

Just what he needed. More poison.

He descended the wall a little, then reached for the grappling hook attached to the side of his backpack. He threw it over the top of the wall, hoping the glass hadn't been spelled to sever steel, then gave the line a tug. Relief hummed through him when the hook and its metal cable held firm.

He climbed up, using the hook as a counterweight so he could stand on the edge of the wall and peer over the broken glass. There was nothing for it. *It's times like these that I really miss the wings.* He rocked back then jumped, flying over the shards and landing in a crouch in the middle of the parapet.

He quickly scanned the walkway. No guards.

Perfect.

This is too easy.

Yeah, well, he wasn't about to discount his good luck...or the fact that he knew the guard rotation. He quickly grabbed the hook and re-coiled the steel cable, attaching it to his pack. Hurrying forward, he reached a door that led inside. From the schematics he'd studied before getting here, this entry should take him down through to the main hall, but who knew how accurate those plans were? Knowing Set, he probably changed the internal alignment on a regular basis just to confuse everyone. He had been a god of chaos, after all.

Despite the urgency that drove him, Azrael took a few extra minutes to check the door for booby-traps. There could be a magical alarm that would be triggered if it was opened at the wrong time, so he decided it was better to wait for a guard to go through it. He checked his watch—one should be patrolling this area in a moment or so.

Settling back in the shadows, he counted five minutes before the portal opened, and a guard stepped through.

The security is appalling.

Then again, Set just might be that overconfident.

The guard sauntered on his way, and Azrael slipped out of his cover and through the door before it shut. He took the stairs quickly, grateful for the billowing torches, so he didn't have to stumble in the dark. He had excellent night vision, but even he couldn't see in the pitch black. Maybe they didn't have electricity in this part of Hell.

Reaching the bottom of the stairs, he strode down the adjoining hallway, heading north. Set's office was meant to be in the middle of the structure.

As he crept along unseen, the little hairs on the back of his neck went up. Like he was being followed.

But no one was there.

What if some of the guards are also invisible?

He shook the thought away. Invisibility magic

generally came at a great price—warrior angels had it instinctively, because they had to get close to their prey. Most demon races didn't have those abilities, however, and buying them cost more than they could afford to pay.

He stepped through a doorway and into a great hall, then quickly backed out a few steps. He thought back over the map he'd memorized—this room didn't exist on it.

Wonderful. One of Set's changes. That, or the spy who'd made the map hadn't been aware of this room when they'd visited.

Either option was highly likely.

He studied the room from the shadowy hall. It reminded him of a museum, with ranks of glass cabinets, each lit from an overhead source. Rows and rows of display cases covered the length of the room, and the glimmer of gold, the shine of precious stones, and the dark pulse of forbidden magics caught his eye.

A treasure room.

Maybe Odin's Orb was stored here.

Stepping cautiously into the chamber, he barely made it five steps before dropping to his stomach. Air whistled over his head, and he looked up to see crossbow bolts slashing overhead to slam into the wall behind him.

Booby traps.

Yay.

Glancing down at his arms, he swore. He was visible again. The spell hadn't even lasted an hour and a half; he must be weaker than he'd thought. Carefully, he inched forward, eyes peeled for further triggers. A low, muttered curse reached him as he approached a glass cabinet full of crystal skulls. Fighting the urge to stop and examine the priceless artifacts, he moved toward the sound.

No.

It was Candy.

She stood next to a display case, her white hair braided and wrapped around her head in a pseudo-crown. Another curse split the air, but he realized it wasn't aimed at him. Her legs seemed to be frozen in place, and she was twisting her torso, growling in frustration.

"Having trouble?" he asked, moving into her eyeline.

She straightened, her mouth dropping open before snapping shut again. "You're *alive*."

He shrugged. "I'm hard to kill."

But she was shaking her head, her gaze roving over him, like she'd seen a ghost. "You shouldn't be alive."

His inner lie-detector pinged. Truth. Well, the truth at least as far as she believed it. Her response told him that she really *had* been trying to kill him. Now her lethal edge made sense: she was another assassin, and only half-human, apparently.

"Sorry to disappoint you," he said.

She snorted, her expression hardening. "Want to help free me?"

He shook his head. "Not a chance." He wasn't about to underestimate her again. Plus, he didn't want any competition. The Orb—and the contract on the god—were his.

He made to move away, but something made him pause.

He couldn't leave her there, trapped, a nice prize for Set to add to his collection.

Don't do it.

He ran a hand through his hair. "Fuck."

If you help her, it's just so that you can keep an eye on her. You can punish her for what she did to you later.

But why did all the 'punishments' that ran through his mind involve both of them naked, and writhing in pleasure?

Sighing, he walked back to her. "I'll help you, but on one condition." He held up a finger.

She glanced up at him, surprise stamped on her features. "Which is?"

"You have to kiss me. Willingly."

He really hadn't just said that. From the look on her face, he had. He was losing his damned mind. But he wanted to taste her again—and not get clawed for the privilege.

She snorted. "I'll get free without your help."

"Before someone else finds you?"

She growled again, the sound sending blood rushing to his groin. *Really bad timing.*

Then her shoulders slumped a little. "Fine, I'll kiss you. But my choice where, when and for how long."

He knew she'd try and weasel out of it, but she'd promised, and a promise to an angel was binding. "Done."

CHAPTER 9

The moment Az uttered the word 'done', a tingle of magic spread over Dru's skin, sinking through her flesh and into her bones. She'd just made a deal—a proper one. It meant she *had* to fulfil her end of the bargain, or something horrible would happen to her. Like her blood would boil, or her skin would melt off. Probably something her imagination couldn't even conceive.

But normal demon deals required blood to seal a bargain.

So, he really is an angel.

The problem with deals—or the benefit, depending on your perspective—was that there were always loopholes. At least she'd been specific when she'd made this one. She'd manage to work something out so that the angel wouldn't get the upper hand.

Worry about it later.

Wasn't that her motto in life?

"How'd you get stuck?" Az asked as he came closer, the muscles on his chest rippling as he moved. He was so alive, so vigorous. Maybe angels *were* immune to Mortus demon toxin, even fallen ones.

"I touched the case." She pointed at the wooden unit behind her in which sat two crystal skulls. Thought to be a myth by humans, it seemed that Set had squirreled them away into his personal collection. They were quite impressive, and also incredibly creepy. Dru was used to seeing dead bodies with their flesh *on*. Naked skeletons were weird, especially ones carved from stone that radiated a low-level hum of dark energy.

"Why?" He crossed his arms over his chest.

"I was avoiding *that*." She pointed with her right hand at the swirling red menace a little behind another cabinet.

Az's eyes widened when he spotted it. "Is that a Devilsgate?"

"I have no idea what it is, but I wasn't about to take my chances with it."

The fiery glow looked a little like a spiral galaxy. It spun above the floor in a hypnotic manner, beautiful in its own way. But unexplained magical lights should be avoided at all costs.

It *probably* was a Devilsgate, but she'd never seen one like this before. If its purpose was to actually teleport someone, it was probably to a really bad place, like Satan's inner lair. That's why she'd side-stepped it without paying too much attention, and had accidentally brushed against the glass of the display unit. Talk about over-the-top security.

Set sure was paranoid.

Az was right next to her now, his body heat caressing her skin. Damn, he was good looking and he smelled *amazing*, like sandalwood. It was lucky she was immune to that kind of thing, courtesy of Trick, or she'd be pressing her nose right up to him.

Then why do you suddenly feel okay with your deal?

I don't.

She was totally going to cheat on it. But it wouldn't hurt her to make out with Hottie McHotpants; at least, it wouldn't hurt anything but her pride.

Her eyes drifted over him. He'd teamed his black T-shirt with black cargo pants, the pockets no doubt filled with all kinds of contraptions. Her fingers itched to liberate a few. She liked gadgets.

"Seems like you messed up big time." He bent down and poked at her legs.

She glared at him. "What did I say about the no-touching rule?"

"How else am I meant to work out what kind of magic has you pinned? I need to feel it."

"Pfft."

More like he needed an excuse to feel her up. But even she had to admit, his touch was entirely businesslike—he didn't prolong the contact, and seemed to pick very specific areas to prod, none of them remotely sexual. Unless he had a shin-fetish.

"Okay, it's just a binding spell. I can't tell if it also unleashed an alarm when it got activated, so we'll get you free and then get moving fast."

"Sure."

She'd certainly move fast once she was freed—away from him.

Opening one of his pants' pockets, he muttered a few words she couldn't make out. Then he grabbed some greenish-colored powder and flung it at her.

"Hey!" She held her hands up in front of her eyes.

Her stomach did a little flip-flop when the glittering powder hit her, and the taste of limes burst to life in her mouth.

"Try to move."

She took a step forward. "Yes!" She fist-pumped the air. She was *free*.

"Great, now let's get going."

"Wait. Get going *together*?" She tightened the straps on her backpack, turning back to glare at the display case. She should steal one of the skulls on principal.

"You owe me that kiss."

"Right."

She hadn't intended that they'd pair up, had wanted to get away from him, but it made a strange kind of sense. At least for now. She could use him to get to the former god, and then ditch him, go in for the kill, and grab the Orb-thingy.

Nice.

And she wouldn't have to worry about the kiss. He hadn't specified that it had to be *soon*. Plus, Dru didn't mind improvisation. She'd learned that, in her line of work, strict adherence to plans could get you killed. Demons were unpredictable, if nothing else.

Carefully, they made their way through the labyrinthine museum, pausing from time to time to admire the strange and deadly artifacts. There was a glowing red crystal scepter that she wanted, even though Az said it was dangerous as Hell: it had bad ju ju or something. That was why she wanted it so bad, but she wasn't foolish enough to touch another display case. She could come back for it later.

Oh, she planned to go wild in here later.

While she'd been impressed with the scepter, he'd muttered continually since spotting a set of scales with a feather resting on one side. It wasn't happy muttering either. "Fucking gods, stealing what doesn't belong to them."

She gathered the item might have been angelic in origin but didn't bother asking him what it did—she'd heard the legends. Weigh your heart against a feather and see which one was heavier. Physics made it obvious: the feather was lighter. But then, magic had a strange way of screwing things up.

Case in point: Dru and Peony.

They were cambions: half-demon/half-human. And cambions were always fucked up, no matter what, because when two demons bred, one side of the genes always won out over the other. Halfbreeds didn't exist. *Except* when you put a human in the mix. Magic didn't seem to like mixing with non-magic.

Az stopped so suddenly she slammed into his back. He half-turned, holding his finger up to his lips.

Oh no, he didn't.

He turned away again, dismissing her.

He totally did.

Normally, she'd have bitch-slapped him—no one shushed her—but something sinuous was sliding through the shadows, a rasping noise accompanying the movement. She stared in its direction, trying to lock onto whatever had made the sound. The small glimpse she'd had indicated scales. Scales were bad.

There was a low hiss, following by a rush of warmth.

Uh-oh. A snake, or a serpent demon of some kind.

A low rumble made the glass in the nearby cabinets

vibrate.

"What the fuck is that?" she whispered, close enough to Az's ear that her breath stirred his hair. Whatever shampoo he used, it smelled delicious. "Wait, what shampoo—"

"I think it's a—"

A roar filled the room, freezing Dru to the spot.

A large, snake-like head shot at them, whip-fast, mouth open wide and filled with razor-sharp teeth.

"—*dragon!*"

They ran.

"How the fuck does he have a dragon in here?" Dru shouted as they darted carelessly past the cabinets, tripping all sorts of alarms and spells. Somehow, she didn't get caught in any. The sound of scales on stone set the hairs on the back of her neck on end.

Az growled. "How the Hell should I know?"

She leaped over a trip-wire and headed for the way she'd entered. Az, barely breathing fast, kept pace next to her. "We need to find cover!"

Dru risked a glance over her shoulder, and her mouth dropped when she saw the dragon easily maneuvering around the cabinets, taking the greatest care not to damage them.

It thinks this is its treasure.

She'd always known the giant legged serpents were hoarders—she just hadn't thought they could be used for security guards.

Sprinting, she didn't see the small step until she tripped over it. "Shit!"

She tried to break her fall, angling herself to land on her side, but was thrown off balance when Az slammed into her. "What the Hell!"

The two of them flailed on the ground, slamming to a halt against a case. Wood groaned, and glass rattled ominously.

The slithering stopped.

Dru took a deep breath. Maybe they were safe.

The air tingled. Looking down, she swallowed.

A large circle surrounded them, drawn in blood, presumably from the figure that had been discarded off to the side, used. The horned head indicated the blood donor had been some sort of demon, but she couldn't tell the species. Her eyes traced over the glyphs. She couldn't make out every symbol, but she could understand enough.

They were screwed.

"We're in a Devilsnare," she muttered.

"What?" Az tried to shove himself upright, but all he managed was to punch her accidentally in the stomach.

She wheezed. "Fuck."

A slow, insulting clapping echoed around the room.

A man stepped into the light, tall and handsome, with dark-brown skin and eyes that glittered like rubies. The dragon twisted into view behind him, wrapping its tail neatly around powerful hind legs, almost like a cat.

"Hades must really want me dead," the man said in a low, melodic voice that spoke of desert sands.

Set.

Dru fought to control her breathing, before shoving Az off her. She stood, the fallen angel following suit. "Oh?"

"A real live angel, and a cambion. And not just any cambion, *the* Death Dealer." Set's expression turned lustful, covetous, like they'd both make great additions to his exhibits. She fought a shudder. Maybe he collected people, as well.

The former god tilted his head toward the discarded corpse. "Well, and someone sent that guy, too. But he wasn't nearly as interesting."

"Death Dealer?" Az muttered.

Dru ignored him. "I didn't know you'd heard of me," she said to Set.

"You know who she is, but you can't get *my* species right?" Az said.

Ego: 1, Az: 0.

"You're an angel." Set rolled his eyes. "What more is there to know?"

"I'm a fallen angel, asshole. No wings."

Dru inspected her nails, like all this was no big deal. Really she was trying to think of a way out of this situation, but she was coming up blank. Devilsnares trapped people—they weren't designed to be escaped.

Come on, think.

The trap encircled both them and the cabinet they had slammed into. Using her peripheral vision, she studied the contents of the display case. A gold ring with a huge glowing emerald sat on a red velvet cushion. A little tag, placed to the front of the cushion, read, 'Hermes' Gift'.

Hermes: messenger for the Greek Gods.

Hrm.

While Set and Az bickered over semantics, Dru slowly reached into her back pocket, finding her multipurpose knife. It wasn't the most ideal tool, but it wasn't like she could grab anything else without garnering too much attention.

The glass on the cabinet next to her was quite thin. The tool should be able to shatter it, provided there weren't any fancy protection spells on it.

Here goes nothing.

Raising her arm, she slammed the knife handle into the glass, raining sharp fragments down on her arms and hands. Little pricks of pain accompanied the glass rain, but she ignored them. She'd heal.

"What are you doing?" Set shouted.

Shoving her hand through the newly made hole, she grabbed the ring. At the moment of contact, knowledge speared into her mind; the magical artifact telling her what it was, and how to use it.

Okay, that's crazy. Her head throbbed, but she could deal with the pain later.

Shoving the band onto her left middle finger, she grabbed Az's hand.

Eyes wild, he shook his head. "No, don't—"

But it was too late. She twisted the ring on her finger.

They vanished.

CHAPTER 10

"What the fuck did you do?" Azrael yelled.

"I got us out of there," she replied.

Candy dropped his arm and stepped away, rubbing her temples. He looked over her shoulder, taking in where she'd teleported them. A cave. At least, that's what he assumed it was: it had rough, natural rock walls, stalactites and a dirt floor. It was humid as well, the air sticky with moisture and the tang of sulfur.

Anger burned though him, bright and hot. "But we were right there! We could have killed him."

"We were in a *Devilsnare*. We couldn't have done anything until it was broken. And he didn't look like he was about to let us out." She shook her head and then winced at the motion.

Anxiety lanced through him, but he pushed the feeling aside. *She doesn't deserve my concern. She's screwed everything up.*

Again.

"Where are we?"

She looked at the ground. "I don't know."

Truth.

"*You don't know?!*"

"This ring was a gift from the former god, Hermes, to one of his lovers. He used to be able to travel around at the blink of an eye. So, he gave her that ability, too."

She was telling the truth about this, too. At least, as far as she knew it.

Teleportation. It wasn't a common magical skill, although a lot of the former 'gods' had been so gifted.

She looked around the cave. "I didn't have a strong enough destination in mind, so it took us here. It's in one of the Hells. Must have been an old rendezvous for the god and his lover."

She hadn't planned where they'd go? The day was just getting better and better.

Why had he agreed to help her?

Oh right. He'd been thinking with his *other* brain.

He studied the cave again. It just looked like a…well, a cave. "How can you tell we're still in Hell?"

She breathed deeply. "The air. I've never been to Heaven, but I've spent enough time in the Human Realm and the various Hells to know the difference. Plus, there's always this low-level hum of magic in the underworld that the Human Realm doesn't have."

Surprise sizzled through him. She was more astute than he had given her credit for. He was still going to take points away from her because of her escape plan. Or lack of one.

He paced around the cave, searching for a way out. "How'd you know the artifact would teleport us?"

"Educated guess."

He spun around. "A *guess*?"

"Well, yeah. I read the label in the display case; it said Hermes. I knew his skills. When I touched it, it gave me the CliffsNotes version of its history and how to use it."

"Do all demon artifacts do that?"

"I don't know. It's not like I go around stealing magical objects all day every day."

"Really?"

"That's for other members of the guild. My abilities lie with knives, not lockpicks." Interesting. He knew that various assassin guilds took on a variety of different roles, but he hadn't really done much research into how they actually operated. That was Raze's job, since he was the CEO of their little company. Azrael was just the muscle.

Candy began to search the cave as well, and together they covered the small chamber relatively quickly. "No booby traps as far as I can see," she said.

"What's your real name?" he asked, coming a stop next to her. He didn't invade her personal space, but was close enough that he could scent jasmine. Fuck, it was a nice change to the rest of the cave.

She sighed. "Does it matter?"

He lowered his voice and leaned forward. "I can call you Candy, but I may make jokes about sucking on you until you melt."

She raised a single eyebrow. "Aren't you an angel?"

"Fallen angel."

"I didn't think you guys did the bedsheet tango."

"Clearly, I make exceptions."

Damn, but her skepticism was hot.

You are such a pervert.

Not really. From the beginning, he'd been honest

about his intentions toward her. It was just too bad she wasn't as interested.

Angels aren't meant to fuck demons.

No, but then, angels weren't meant to fall, either. And she was a cambion, which surely had to count for something. *Probably something bad, knowing my luck.*

He continued to stare at her until finally she gave him a resigned look. "It's Drucilla—but I prefer to be called Dru."

"Dru." He tasted the word on his tongue, decided he liked it. It suited her.

She narrowed her eyes. "Shall we get moving?"

He glanced around. "To where? Does the ring work again?"

"Grab my arm."

An invitation to touch her delectable self? He wasn't going to say no to that. He reached out, gripping her wrist, and ran his thumb in a small circle over her pulse.

She twisted out of his grasp. "Stop that."

"You told me to touch you."

"I didn't say for you to feel me up in the process."

He frowned. "You and I have very different definitions of what 'feeling up' entails."

She shook her head, and then held her arm out again. "Behave, or I'll remove some body parts of yours that I am sure you're *very* attached to."

"Threats. I like that in a woman." Although, he did like his balls more, and he figured those would be her target.

"You're fucked up, you know that?"

He wrapped his hand around her wrist, careful to not apply too much pressure. Her bones felt delicate, which contrasted with everything else about her. "Old news."

She lifted her left hand and wiggled the finger with the ring on it. "The emerald isn't glowing anymore."

He stared at the piece of jewelry, at the giant-ass stone that would be worth a king's ransom in the Human Realm. "How do you activate it?"

She twisted it around on her finger. Her hands were slender and sinewy, like a musician's, but calloused like a fighter's.

Azrael waited. Blinked. Waited a bit longer. "We're still here."

"Thank you for pointing that out, Captain Obvious."

He ignored her tone.

She stared thoughtfully at the stone. "Maybe it only works once it's glowing again."

He let go of her wrist, even though he was enjoying the contact. He had other things to worry about, namely getting back to Set's castle and getting that Orb. "So, we're stuck here?"

She met his gaze, her gray eyes calm. "For the time being."

"Give it to me, and I'll try." He held out his hand.

Dru stared at him for a moment and he thought she would refuse, but surprise sizzled through him when she tugged on the ring, frowning when it didn't budge. "It's stuck."

Truth.

"Let me try." He reached out and grasped the ring with his thumb and forefinger, but it was glued to her finger.

Panic lit her gray eyes for a moment, and she bit her lip. "It won't move."

"Maybe it needs to be glowing to be removed," Azrael said, more to placate her than anything else. If the ring couldn't be taken off, it meant he was entirely dependent on her when it came to getting back to Set.

Great.

He turned away and began checking the cave again. She did the same. After a few minutes, she called out, "Over here."

His boots crunched on the dirt floor as he walked toward her. "What?"

She shut her eyes, tilting her chin up toward the stalactites. "Can you feel it?"

All he could feel was the growing erection in his cargo pants. He quickly readjusted himself while she had her eyes closed. "No."

"Did you even try?"

"Since I have no idea what I am meant to be feeling..." He let the sentence hang, and then dropped his gaze to her breasts, just to irritate her, although the view *was* good. However, even his libido would admit that freedom was better than sex. At least, at this exact point in time.

"Eyes up," she said. "There's a breeze. Can you feel it?"

He held his arms out, palms toward the walls of the cave. A cooler stream of air that eased some of the oppressive humidity breathed over them. "Where's it coming from?"

Carefully, she picked her way forward, stopping at the wall. "Here."

"There's a wall there."

She slashed him a look. "I think it's a hidden door."

He snorted, but came up next to her.

"This was a rendezvous spot for a god," she said. "He was probably careful to hide his tracks. I know I would be, especially if the Great Culling had started." She made the Culling sound like it had been a bad thing. Sympathy for deposed gods?

She is *half-demon*.

"The gods deserved it, you know," Azrael said as he searched the wall for cracks or seams.

"*Of course* they did. Just like demons deserve to die just cos they're demons."

The sarcasm, it burned.

She ran her hands over the stone, her clever fingers seeking the door's trigger. "But you're an angel, so you see the world in two ways."

"What do you mean by that?"

"Good and evil. Two extremes, and nothing else."

He used to think like that, he wouldn't deny it, to her or anyone. Not so much anymore. He'd learned in the past few months that there was a lot more to people than met the eye. He'd rubbed shoulders with demons he wouldn't mind having a drink with, and had sex with humans he would have viewed as inferior not long ago. Add that to the way the Darts had been treated by the supposed good guys...

Yeah, he was developing a whole new world view.

Thinking of the Darts...he swept his mind out, trying to connect with Raze. Nothing. Seraphina? Just a gray mist. Finally, he tried Yael, but failed to make mental contact again. Isolated. For the first time in centuries, he was truly alone.

His eyes tracked to Dru. Well, not *entirely* alone.

"Got it!" She stepped back and pumped a fist in the air just as the door swung inward. She slung her pack off one shoulder, then brought it around to her front, rummaging through it for something. A second later, she had a flashlight out and on, and twisted her pack back into position.

He crowded her, peering through the opening, but it was pitch black and even his eyesight couldn't make out anything.

"I'll go first," Dru said.

He moved backward slightly. "Be my guest."

She flicked a glance over her shoulder. "No macho bullshit about you being a guy and a *fallen* angel and thus stronger than me?"

He waved a hand in the air. "If you want to get murdered first, go right ahead. I'll learn from your mistakes."

She gave a muffled laugh before her expression hardened. A second later, she was in the passageway, the beam of light slicing through the darkness to show more stone walls, a carved ceiling, and the same dirt floor. There wasn't much of anything else.

It's probably a trap.

Yeah, but he didn't really have another other options, especially since Dru was wearing the ring that had brought them here. Teleportation wasn't in his skillset. Quickly, he followed her, then cursed under his breath as the stone door ground closed behind him.

She spun round. "You didn't prop it open?"

Her flashlight momentarily blinded him and he held up a hand to protect his eyes. "Uh, that would be a no."

She shook her head and turned back. "Let's hope this

leads somewhere, then."

"You managed to open it the last time."

He thought she might have murmured something like 'through luck', but he chose not to dwell on it.

A few seconds later, a new wall loomed in front of them. She handed him the torch. "Let's see how this one goes."

She ran her hands over the stone.

"Never thought I'd envy a wall," he said.

Dru didn't even pause in her examination. "You fallen angels really take your status literally, don't you?"

"And you cambions are stubborn as Hell."

"It comes with the territory." She grinned at him, and fuck, it felt like his heart might stop. Her face lost its natural guardedness, and she became the most beautiful woman he'd ever seen, her gray eyes glowing, and her lush mouth welcoming. And it did nothing to conceal the hint of wickedness that lurked beneath the surface — the part about her that he liked the most.

He was so screwed.

CHAPTER 11

Opening concealed doorways wasn't exactly Dru's forte, but she'd managed to do two in about fifteen minutes. No doubt that meant her good luck was going to expire sooner rather than later.

Although, Sylvester would be proud of her. He was the only other cambion—aside from Peony—who worked for the guild, and he was an expert at breaking and entering. Or, as he called it, visiting and pilfering.

"Nice." Az came to stand next to her, looking out into the chamber beyond their hidden walkway. It was shadowy, but light was filtering in from somewhere.

Dru was careful to ensure that there were no traps on the other side of the door before she stepped into the new cavern. This was bigger than the one they'd arrived in, and the air was cooler, slightly fresher. That might indicate they were closer to an exit.

Probably just hopeful thinking.

She moved the flashlight beam around carefully, hoping to highlight any warnings.

Nothing.

Just dirt and stone floors, rocky walls, and humidity.

She breathed deep, and thought she detected the tang of a water source. There was probably a spring in here somewhere, which accounted for the damp air.

"It still reeks of sulfur here," Az said.

She hated how his voice made something hot coil deep within her, like she wanted to strip naked and get him to follow suit. She'd have to give her libido a stern talking to. "We're in Hell. The smell kind of comes with the territory." She barely even noticed it anymore.

"Yeah, well. My trip to Inferno was my first visit to your lovely home. And it wasn't what I was expecting."

"I don't live in Inferno. But it doesn't normally look like that. I think Set has a pretty big influence on how that part of the realm appears."

Which meant that Set was more than just the common sorcerer word said he'd been demoted to. But then, her visit to his little 'keep' had already clued her in on that— he had a dragon protecting his hoard, magical barriers embedded into the walls, *and* could make a crazy-powerful Devilsnare.

All those things pointed to the asshole still being a god, even though they weren't meant to exist anymore.

Stepping out into the cavern, her gaze roamed the space. *There.* The light was emanating from a side tunnel to her left. She started toward it, Az trailing behind. For a mercenary Hell-bent on getting home as quickly as possible, he sure let her make a lot of the decisions. She wasn't sure if his complacency annoyed her or not.

She didn't like passive men.

You don't like him.

Yeah, well, she still owed him that stupid kiss.

"Do you have any idea where we are in Hell?"

She shook her head. "We're in a cave. There's caves all over Hell." They added to the atmosphere of the place, or something.

"Are we far from the exit, do you think?" He came to a stop beside her.

"What do I look like, a speleologist?"

He shot her an amused look. "Big word for a mercenary."

She ignored him and kept walking. Soon, the light had grown intense enough that she didn't need her flashlight anymore. She tucked it away in her pack, so her hands were free. Just in case.

Az squatted down suddenly, and Dru noticed that the tunnel's dirt floor was glittering now, like the surface was made up of crushed gems.

She bent down to see. They were emeralds; tiny—each one bare millimeters across—but they were worth a fortune in every realm. Pulling her backpack across her chest, she rummaged in it and drew out a velvet bag, then scooped a handful of the stones into it.

Az watched her. "What are you doing?"

"Isn't it obvious?"

"They are tiny."

She pulled the drawstring shut, then tucked the emeralds away. "But still worth something."

"They're just Hell stones."

Trust an angel to be so dismissive. Then again, she'd been to his house. The guy was loaded. And Dru had a debt she still needed to pay off.

She rose to her feet and continued down the tunnel. A minute or so later, they emerged into the open. Dru stopped, blinking into the light. Craggy stone rose into the air before them, jagged rocks with razor-sharp edges that jutted into the smog-shrouded sky. A small path wound away from the cave entrance, making her wonder what else used the place.

"At least it's not nighttime."

Dru flicked Az a glance. "Hell doesn't have a sun. In some places, it's always daytime; in others, perpetual darkness."

She had no idea what realm they were in; it wasn't like there was a sign. Turning back to the cave, she checked out the small opening in the rockface. Barely wide enough for two humanoid shapes side-by-side. The bedrock was basalt, lined with veins of quartz.

As she studied their exit point, the cave mouth vanished.

"No!"

Jogging back, she ran her hands over the spot where the opening had disappeared, pounding on it with a closed fist when she realized it was sealed over with magic.

Stone. It looked and felt like stone.

"What are you doing?"

"The cave is sealed. We can't get back in."

Az stuck a thumb through his backpack strap. "That's not a bad thing, right? There wasn't anything in the cave we wanted."

"Are you crazy? It had *shelter*."

"Hmph."

When you didn't know which realm of Hell you were in, any safe harbor was welcome. Sure, she didn't know what the cave was used for—or by *whom*—normally, but if the only entrance vanished from sight every time someone left, it was unlikely to have been occupied all that regularly.

Which meant it had probably been relatively safe.

Hence a former god had used it for a love-nest.

She shook her head, annoyed at herself, at Az, and at Trick, for agreeing to let her go on this stupid mission. *Simple assassination, my ass. This Orb-thingy had better be worth it.*

"Let's go. We'll need to find somewhere else to camp," she said.

"Camp? We're going to find a Devilsgate and get back to Set's lair. Or use that ring."

She stopped walking and turned to stare at the angel. "Do you honestly think there are Devilsgates just hovering all over Hell?"

He shrugged. "Why not? They're called Devilsgates, and they aren't that hard to summon."

"You make one, then."

"I'm an *angel*."

"Right."

"So why don't you think that we will be able to find a Devilsgate soon?"

He honestly looked surprised.

This is what you get for teaming up with a godsdamned angel.

"Because Hell is meant to keep people *in*. It doesn't want its denizens leaving and causing turmoil between the other circles—and gods-forbid—the Human Realm." How long had this guy been fallen?

"But there are plenty of demons in the Human Realm."

"Ones that can pass for human, or who have paid for spells that hide their true identities. The Hell overlords don't want the supernatural world exposed to humanity."

She was beginning to think that his fall had been recent. Like, *really* recent.

"So we're stuck here?" His caramel skin went a shade or so paler.

"Until the ring glows again, yep." And she had no idea how long that would take.

"Fine. Let's get moving then. See if we can learn where we are."

Fat chance of that, but she did want to get moving. Dru didn't like being out in the open in Hell, especially when she didn't know which circle she was in. She was more familiar with Tartarus' idiosyncrasies, so if they were there, she could deal with the surprises better, but each circle had its own terrors. Some were better than others.

Or less worse.

They headed down the track—this one not made out of gemstones, but regular gravel—and she was careful not to brush up against any of the stone outcrops jammed in on either side. Not only did the edges look sharp enough to slice through skin, sometimes the rock hid beings that lived off the rare and stupid flesh that got too close.

The only sounds were their boots crunching on the path, and the atmosphere steadily became oppressive— gone was the humidity of the cave, replaced by a feeling of dread that dwelled deep within a person's hindbrain.

"Do you fee—?"

"Sssh." Dru held up a hand as she came to a stop.

The path terminated a few yards in front of her, leading toward a rocky plateau, enclosed on all sides by sheer rock walls. They'd been led here, like rats in a maze.

A trap.

White sticks were scattered over the plateau's surface, bundles of twisted branches.

"They're not branches," she whispered to herself.

As she looked closer, she could see the twisted and snapped bones, the screaming skulls, and the scattered horns.

They were the bleached remains of previous travelers.

Fuck.

CHAPTER 12

Dru was muttering profanities under her breath. If she was worried, Azrael probably should be, too.

The path was barely wide enough for them both, but he pressed on, looking over her shoulder as he followed her.

They were standing right in front of a graveyard.

White bones of numerous demon species were spread over the surface of the rocky plateau, a number of skulls staring sightlessly at God-knew-what, femurs of all lengths pointing obscenely toward the sky.

Azrael might be an assassin and a former warrior, but he did not delight in death. Nor in the loss of sentient life, not unless it was necessary. Even demon life. And this place didn't have the feel of a ritual cemetery, it felt offensive.

"What is this place?" he asked.

"Can't you tell?" Dru said quietly. "It's someone's dinner table."

"What would leave remains like this here?"

She unsheathed a knife. "Something big or lots of

somethings that don't care."

"That is not helpful."

"It could be any number of Hell-dwellers. There are some primordial beings who still roam the realms. And most demons are carnivorous. It could even be a clan's hunting grounds. A pack of demons could take down a Toron demon." She waved a hand at the horned skull closest to them, the engraved teeth a tell-tale as to its species.

Torons were built like Neanderthals; sturdy, strong, and muscular, but they stood around eight feet tall. They were ferocious fighters, so whoever killed one had to be powerful themselves.

The Orb was looking further and further out of his grasp.

"Is there a way out?" he asked.

"You're the angel."

"Doesn't make me omnipotent."

"Maybe you need to tell your P.R. department that."

Normally, he'd happily continue the debate, but this wasn't the time or place. "We need to leave."

"No shit."

The tiny hairs on the back of his neck stood on end. "*Now.*"

Some of his urgency must have laced his voice, because she gave him a serious look before turning back to the plateau. "I can't see any paths that lead out of here. And the one we just travelled didn't have any branches. It just leads back to the cave, where the opening is closed."

No, that path had been a one-way ticket to a feast.

And Azrael didn't plan on being the main course.

"How's the ring going?" he asked.

They both glanced down at the dull emerald. "Same as before."

So, teleportation was off the cards. At the moment, at least.

Hopefully the ring would recharge soon.

Dru stepped out onto the plateau and paused, as if waiting for a trap to spring. Nothing. Not even a soft breeze. With a sigh of relief, Azrael followed her into the boneyard.

As they walked, they dodged skeletons, careful not to step on any remains. He didn't believe in desecrating the dead. *Although*…kneeling down, he inspected a long bone that had been snapped in two. It was marred with sharp indentations.

"Teeth marks," he murmured.

Aside from being cracked open for marrow, there were no real signs of butchering—no clean cuts that indicated the use of a blade. Whatever had been eating, it was using its claws and teeth.

Nasty claws.

Very sharp teeth.

They were halfway across the plateau when he spotted it. An opening.

He hurried toward the gap, only to be almost jerked off his feet. Dru had a death grip on his backpack, holding him in place. She was stronger than she looked.

"Where are you going?" she whispered.

"Looks like there is an exit." He pointed.

She was quiet for a moment. "There's one on the other side, too."

"You check one, I'll check the other." But as soon as he

said it, dread crawled in the pit of his stomach. They shouldn't split up.

"Are you sure that's a good idea?"

"No."

He turned around, her hand falling away from his pack, and studied the other exit. Another tiny gap in the sheer rockface. And he had no idea where either one led. Right into the monster's lair, for all he knew.

Dru rubbed her forearms. "I'm getting a really bad feeling."

He didn't want to admit it, but— "Same."

"Shall we check each one out together?" she asked.

He started to speak, but his voice died to nothing as he spotted movement on the edges of the walls. Shadows wove over the rockface, roiling down until they reached the plateau floor.

"I don't think we're alone anymore." He drew out two short swords from sheaths on his backpack and dropped into a fighting stance. Distant screams and growls grew rapidly closer as the things crawling over the rock came closer. They moved as a single mass, their timing so perfect he had trouble making out what they actually looked like, even though they were only five hundred yards or so away.

"Do you know what they are?" he asked.

Dru was silent. She slammed a magazine into a gun then withdrew a knife with her free hand. He wasn't into guns, having never needed them before, but maybe he should change his mind. He could at least take out an enemy at a distance, then, rather than having to wait for them to get up close and personal.

Close-in kills were the angel way—but he wasn't a full

angel anymore.

He turned back to the horde. They were not an attractive race. The creatures were short and stocky, with disproportionate heads and torsos, and elongated arms and legs. They had green-gray skin and flyaway greasy hair.

And there were a lot of them.

"Reynard's Imps," Dru muttered.

"Was that a curse? Or what these things are?"

She positioned herself so she was back-to-back with him. "What they are."

"There's different types of imps?"

"There's different types of everything. But this species only lives in Sheol."

"And how do you know about them?" She didn't strike him as a documentary lover, if there even were documentaries on this kind of thing. There were no doubt books.

She kept her voice low. "We have one at the guild. Nasty piece of work. He was sold by his clan."

Slavery.

He didn't know why it surprised him. Demons were demons, after all. And humans had done the same thing—still did it, if one were to believe the news reports. But the idea of owning a sentient creature…it was anathema to angels.

Although, he was beginning to wonder if every member of his kind thought the same way.

The imps were closing in quickly, howling as if anticipating victory. It was only a matter of seconds before they would be swarmed. Despite the imps' synchronized movements, making them eerily appear as one entity, he could discern the individual features of the nearest: sharp black eyes, pointed teeth, and clawed hands. They were also naked as the day they were born, the males clearly excited about the prospect of food.

I really could have lived without noticing that.

Gunshots exploded, triggering high-pitched screams amongst the imps' howls.

He didn't look back to see how they handled Dru's attack.

A second later, three imps launched themselves at him, claws extended, faces twisted in snarls of rage. His blades moved of their own accord, centuries of training rising to the fore. His mind was almost blank as he slashed hands, sliced necks, and cut at the legs of the imps. Blood and gore sprayed over his face, arms, and chest. He spat out a mouthful of dark blood, his sword deflecting another attack, but the moment's distraction cost him—pain burst in his cheek as an imp's claws raked at him.

"Fuck."

The imp hissed at the contact and withdrew.

Odd.

"We're screwed," Dru said, still firing.

"There's too many of them," he agreed. But he didn't want to die here.

With a series of howls, the horde seemed to swell, converging on them in a wave of bodies. Azrael slipped on a puddle of blood, crashing to the ground. Imps leaped on him, and he struggled to fight them off. Stinging pain ricocheted through him as the imps sliced him with their claws...yet they screamed whenever they drew his blood.

Little black eyes glared at him, malice and hunger howling from their depths.

Lifting an arm, Azrael flung the nearest two imps away, but another two claimed their place. One sank sharp teeth into his calf. *Damn, that hurts.*

In the corner of his vision, a green glow caught his attention.

Dru had her gun trained on the imps, her knife hand slashing out with brutal effect. He bucked to his knees, dislodging more imps. He reached out with hands covered in blood—his and the imps'—grabbed her wrist, and twisted the ring on her finger.

"What are you—?"

They disappeared.

CHAPTER 13

Dru's arm lashed out, her blade ready to sink into the flesh of an imp, when she lost her balance and stumbled forward, knife dropping to the ground. Az clung to her left arm. Drawing another gun with her left hand, she shoved the weapon up blindly. But the leaping imp had vanished. As had his nearby friends.

No more rock plateau.

Wait. Were those *trees?*

What the Hell?

She had been seconds away from being swarmed by imps. Az had already fallen, covered in the little assholes, although he'd still somehow managed to fight them off. But despite his ability, and hers, she'd been certain they were both dead. And dinner.

"What happened?" She was panting slightly, whether from surprise, exertion or a little of both, she wasn't entirely sure.

Maybe it was relief.

"I saw that the ring was glowing," Az said. "And I turned it."

She breathed deep, trying to calm her racing heart and get her lungs under control. She was an assassin—fear was not meant to be part of her repertoire. That she'd lost it, even for a moment…

So what if they'd come close to being a snack for a horde of imps? They'd lived, and she'd taken down a lot of the bastards in the process. She shouldn't have lost her training.

Plus, Az had no doubt been just as effective. Killing demons, was, after all, an angel thing. And he didn't look too badly off from the battle, despite being taken to the ground.

They'd teleported from weak daylight to beneath a smooth night sky, the area surrounding them devoid of any about-to-attack creatures. And they were in the middle of a forest, the trees short and scraggly, the underbrush rich with sounds. The track they were on was comprised of crushed grass and broken twigs, and the air held the unmistakable tang of sulfur.

So, they were in Hell still…but *where*?

She pulled her wrist out of Az's grasp and picked up her fallen weapon, cleaning it off on her shirt. The angel dropped back to his knees, face creased with pain. In the poor light, the wet gleam of blood was visible on his clothing.

"They used you as a chew toy," she muttered, dropping to one knee.

She checked the ring on her finger. The stone was dull again. So, they were stuck here, wherever here was, at least for a little while. She took off her pack and rummaged in it for some bandages, ones spelled to be impervious to any kind of harm. Once they were on, they would stay put until the wound was closed. Handy.

As she withdrew her supplies, she wondered how long it had been between the first and second use of the ring. Perhaps it powered up on a regular cycle. She hadn't checked her watch.

Idiot.

You have been a little busy.

No excuse. The ring might be their only ticket out of here, and eventually, back to the guild. Every second that counted down might mean they were closer to returning to Inferno and Set, and finishing her damned assignment. Although, she didn't really want to sit down and have the 'I failed' meeting with Trick, especially not if Az beat her to the kill, or someone else succeeded first.

She took note of the time now, cursing herself.

"What are you doing?" Az asked.

"Helping your sorry ass."

"I–uh…thanks."

"Where's the worst wound?" Angels must have super-healing abilities—he had survived her toxin easily enough, after all—so she should only need to attend to his nastiest injuries to give them time to heal undisturbed.

"My calf."

She moved until she was next to his lower leg; blood still seeped from it, shiny and black in the evening light. "It's already healing. Guess you don't need it cleaned."

Infection probably wasn't too much of an issue when you were immortal.

He made a grunting sound she took to be assent, so she wrapped a bandage around his leg, tying it off with a knot. Probably not how Peony would have done it, but it wasn't like they shared trade secrets.

You really should have spoken to Trick about her little 'task' before you left.

Peony was a big girl, she could handle herself.

Your soft-hearted sister can look after herself?

Yeah, well, she hadn't spoken to him, either way. And that made her a terrible sibling, she knew. But there hadn't been time for her to mention casually to her slave-master that holding an angel prisoner was a bad idea, or that having her sister look after him was even worse. Trick didn't take well to his decisions being questioned, even if he wanted to screw her silly. He was able to separate sex from work. Surprisingly.

He'd probably have Peony locked in the cell with the angel for tattling.

Anyway, if truth be told, her sister needed to try and solve this one on her own. She needed the experience, and the angel *was* injured. And if the problem wasn't fixed by the time Dru got back, she could take care of it, then.

"So, any idea where we are now?" Az asked, breaking her thoughts.

"Hell, somewhere. Not where we were before."

"And the gold medal for the Obvious Games goes to you."

Hey, he was Captain Obvious earlier. She scowled. "I don't see you offering any opinions."

She swung her pack back on, stood and changed the magazine in her gun. As she did so, she studied the small clearing further, looking for a way out, a clue as to where they were. The forest trail led out into the woodland at either end, but she had no idea which direction it travelled. Looking up, she frowned. Starless. Shame. She might have been able to recognize a constellation or two.

No sun and no moon made it hard to orient oneself in Hell. Which was probably the point.

Always keep the denizens off guard.

Az took a few deep breaths before he too got to his feet, wincing as he put weight on his left leg. "Fuck, those creatures have sharp teeth."

His wound *had* looked like someone had cleanly sliced off a nice fillet.

"Metcalf's favorite method of killing is apparently biting out his victim's throat," Dru said, as much to herself as to Az. "Gross and kind of messy, but that's how he prefers it." And it had certainly given the asshole a reputation.

He raised an eyebrow. "Who is Metcalf?"

"The Reynard's Imp at the guild." Seriously, was it that hard to follow along? Maybe the angel had suffered more blood loss than she'd thought.

Her eyes scanned the trees; she had the feeling they were being watched. By what, or by whom, she had no idea.

She sighed.

She so wasn't prepared for this mission.

So much for the 'get in, make the kill, get the treasure, get out' approach.

Dru should never have let Trick manipulate her into doing it. And all for nothing, as it turned out, because Az was still alive. His friends wouldn't have come after a rival guild, not since their buddy had lived. There was no need for her to lay low.

Although, Az might have hunted her down just on principle.

"Uh, Dru?" Az's voice was low.

"Yes?"

"We aren't alone."

He nodded at the tree line, and the cloaked figures who had stepped out while she'd been staring at the path. Great. So much for her situational awareness. The lack of sleep must be getting to her. She hadn't had a nap in about three days.

The closest figure threw back his hood, exposing a face that was as classically handsome as a Greek sculpture. He had long black hair that was tied back in a man-bun, with gray eyes and pale green skin, the color of unripe olives.

For the second time that day, her stomach dropped.

She'd thought the imps were bad.

But this was worse.

So much worse.

"You are trespassing." The demon's voice was low, melodic, but she caught the sinister undertones.

She held the gun to her side, out of the demon male's line of sight.

"We are but travelers," Az said, holding up his bloodied palms.

He has no idea what species we are talking to. If he did, he'd be hightailing it out of here. But she wasn't running away, either.

"You come here covered in gore, and you say you are but travelers?"

She could understand his skepticism.

"We were attacked by imps. Reynold's or something?" Az glanced at her, an eyebrow quirked.

"Reynard's Imps," she clarified, quietly.

The speaker's eyes locked on her. "Your claim is patently false. They are in Sheol; we are in Inferno."

Inferno? So they'd managed to get back to the right realm—but they were a long way from Set's little slice of paradise.

"We teleported here," the angel said.

Why here? she wondered. He was the one who twisted the ring, so it was his destination that they should have gone to. Not here. Not the last place in any of the realms she'd ever want to be. *Aside from back on that plateau.*

"Then teleport out. You, however," he kept his gaze on Dru, "you can stay."

"Uh, I'm really happy to leave as well," she said.

The less time she spent around these demons, the better for her. The better for *all* of them.

"She's the teleporter," Az said. "So where she goes, I go."

Fool. He shouldn't have said that.

The demon's gaze sharpened, became more speculative. "Then you are free to come with us."

"We'll just wait here, and then we'll teleport out, if that's okay," Dru said. She really didn't want to go anywhere with these guys.

The speaker—Speaker, she nicknamed him—smiled, a cold, reptilian expression. "Ah, but I insist."

Within moments, they were surrounded by figures in brown cloaks, their cowls drawn up and covering their faces. She couldn't tell if they were all men, or if there were some women in the mix, but from what she knew of this race of demons, there was unlikely to be a female among them.

Sexist out-of-date assholes, the lot of them.

"Please, come with us." Speaker waved a hand, as if he were welcoming them to a medieval court.

"Well, since we can hardly refuse…" Dru murmured, and went to take a step forward. She tucked her gun back into its holster; she could get off a few shots easily enough, but there were still too many of them, and Az was injured.

"Mind being my crutch? My leg still hurts." The fallen angel spoke loudly while he slung an arm over her shoulders. The gesture earned him a glacial glare from Speaker, the false cheer vanishing from the demon's eyes. Back to the emotionless expression he went, the one that spoke of cold calculation and torture chambers.

"Of course," Dru said, like her no-touching rule didn't exist. For Az, she supposed she'd started making exceptions when they wound up in Hermes' cave. He hadn't died from her poison, so he might be safe from her. Whether or not she was safe from him, well, that was another problem for a later time.

They started along the trail, the demons keeping pace alongside them through the woodland. She had a feeling they'd be attacked if she even so much as sneezed. *Good thing I don't have hay fever.*

She was careful to keep her expression neutral, but inside she chafed at the physical contact from Az, just not in the normal way. Not in her usual touch-me-and-I will-slice-your-throat kind of way. No, his arm resting on her shoulders, and the sheer warmth and solidarity of him beside her—it was doing things to her that she didn't like and didn't *want*.

Desire.

Her body was growing warm and hungry for a damned fallen angel. And it was awakening at the worst possible time. Lust wasn't something she was all that familiar with; not when it always ended disastrously.

"So," Az whispered in her ear. "What kind of demons are these?"

She shot him a look. How could he not know about one of the most feared species of demon within all the Hells?

Then again, it wasn't like this lot were well known for visiting the Human Realm. Angels would have little to do with them otherwise.

"They're Mortus demons."

Chapter 14

What the Hell kind of species is a Mortus demon? Az wondered.

The way Dru had delivered the news made him think he should know.

The term Mortus did ring a faint bell. More information would come to him, he just had to wait. There were so many memories crammed into his skull about demonic breeds that it took time for the information to filter through. The first decade or two of his training had involved learning about every known species there was—mostly their vulnerabilities, so he could decide on the best tactics to use against them.

Then he'd spent the next century learning how to fight and implement those tactics.

Azrael leaned heavily on Dru's shoulder. His weakness was as much for practicality as for show. One of those damned imps had taken a chunk out of his calf, and while it was healing already, it still hurt like crazy. Better for these new demons to think him badly injured and unable to fight.

The fellow who was leading them through the forest was attractive, Azrael supposed, if you liked that kind of thing; he could pass for human easily enough, except for the greenish skin. But there was something about him that radiated evil—the real kind, not the he's-a-bad-person kind. The torture-kittens-for-fun kind. The descended-from-a-Hell-ruler kind.

Not the kind of guy you wanted to date, or to stand behind you, or really be anywhere *near* you.

The leader kept looking over his shoulder, his eyes raking over Dru with an almost proprietary gleam. Tension radiated from her, her muscles clenching under Azrael's weight. Whatever these demons were, they weren't good. Not if someone like Dru was worried about them. He wished his memory would supply the information on the Mortus; he really needed to know.

"These Mortus demons. What kind of breed are they?" he whispered, his lips hovering a little too close to the shell of her ear. She smelled like flowers still.

Her reply was barely louder than an exhaled breath. "My kind."

He stumbled.

Had she just implied—?

"But you don't look anything like them…"

She grimaced and held out her hand, letting him see her claws. "Similar enough in certain ways."

He stared at her long fingers, her message sinking home, and absently rubbed a hand over his chest. The trees standing sentinel along the trail were slowly thinning out, and he tried to determine where they were headed.

Mortus demons are toxic.

Long-forgotten memories resurfaced, his former tutor's voice rolling through his mind. *"The Mortus are some of the most feared demons in Inferno. Directly descended from Satan himself, they are a brutal feudal society with little care for life other than that of another Mortus demon. Their skin is toxic to the touch and can even kill an angel. Beware of this species, and only engage if absolutely necessary."*

They were said to emerge from their little area of Inferno only rarely, and only at Satan's bidding or for their own commercial interests.

So how on earth was a Mortus-human cambion even *possible*?

The combination made no sense—especially if a Mortus' toxin was deadly enough to take out even an angel. A human would have no chance of surviving conception.

The party emerged from the woodland, and the head-honcho paused for a moment. Azrael rose to his full height briefly, taking in the scene before him. The forest trail led to a gravel crossroads, with paths that headed off to his left and right, and a third that ventured straight forward, into the intricately carved mouth of a huge cavern.

Another cave. Just my luck.

Sentries stood guard along the roadway, and even he could do the math. He and Dru were outnumbered. At this stage, it was only about twenty-to-one—better odds than the imps had been, but these demons were of a similar height and build to a regular human. He doubted they would survive long if they tried to run. Not that he *could* run right now. But in another hour…

They began walking again, this time toward the

cavern, which had been carved to resemble an open maw, complete with jagged rocky teeth and an undulating tongue.

Inventive.

"What do you see?" Dru asked quietly.

"Lots of guards, crossroads. We're badly outnumbered."

She exhaled slowly.

While the sentries barely batted an eyelid at their presence, he could sense their curiosity about the new visitors. And for some reason, Azrael didn't think he was the main attraction. Sure, Dru was smoking hot in terms of feminine appeals, but the evaluating glances told him it was more than that.

Maybe female Mortus demons are rare.

If that was the case, they were both royally screwed, because he couldn't leave without her. And if females of the species weren't common, then the Mortus demons were unlikely to just let her walk out of their clutches. Not now they had new breeding stock.

Well, you can't do anything about it right now.

No. He should be memorizing the layout, trying to work out how the two of them could escape. So far, it was pretty easy: follow the road-slash-tongue.

They were still in the main entrance, which descended for a couple hundred yards before the first torches appeared. *No electricity.* Then again, it was Hell. What was he expecting?

After another half a minute, their group stopped at a dead end. Writing was etched on the wall in front of him, and it reminded him of an ancient angelic dialect, one he'd never been taught, but had seen. Lucifer was meant to be the fallen angel, not Satan, so why did the Mortus demons have angelic text?

The lead demon turned to face them. "Only the woman comes with us. You will wait here."

Azrael didn't move, keeping his arm loosely around Dru's shoulders. "Sorry, but no."

The man's gray eyes flashed. "You have no say here."

"He goes where I go," Dru said. "You don't like it, try and convince me to change my mind." She levelled a look of pure malice at the demon, her gray eyes turning an inky black, her humanity stripped away to reveal the heart of the monster that lurked within. It surprised Azrael so much he almost leaned away from her.

A faint pulse of pure evil swirled through her, but it was gone a moment later.

Does she know what she did?

Because it was scary as Hell.

And also kind of sexy.

Something is seriously wrong with you.

He was an angel—that heartbeat of evil should have had him turning his back on the woman, condemning her to death. Back in his days among the Darts, that tiny moment of demonic rage would have signed her execution order. Now, though, all it did was the opposite. Because he understood what drove humans and demons better now that he wasn't winged. Most weren't just two-dimensional beings capable of only death and pain. Dru *controlled* the demon that resided within her, and was smart enough to let it loose when she needed its power.

And there was nothing wrong with using the tools you were born with.

The Mortus demon stared at them for another minute

before tilting his head to the side. "Your bravado does you justice."

"It isn't bravado if I'm willing to back it up," Dru replied.

"This way." The demon's mouth tightened in a line that implied disbelief. *His loss*, Azrael thought. If the demon couldn't see he was playing with an assassin, when a knife inevitably slid between his ribs, that was on him.

Azrael had already learned that lesson the hard way.

I'm never underestimating a woman in a tight dress again.

He'd thought he could see all her charms, but he'd been wrong and he'd nearly died for it. Oh, he'd healed, but he still had the scars, and even he could admit how close he'd come to dying.

He didn't know why he hadn't lost that battle, but he wasn't about to ignore his good luck.

CHAPTER 15

They were led away from the cave entrance and through a series of tunnels that appeared identical in nature. The tunnels were largely devoid of artwork, but some kind of alien writing was carved into almost every surface; Dru had no idea what it said, or what it meant, but the script gave her the heebie-jeebies. Like it wasn't intended to ever be seen by her eyes.

She tried to keep the lefts and rights in order in a mental map, but had the feeling they were deliberately being led in circles so that they would have trouble escaping later, if they tried. She was *sure* they'd travelled down this corridor before, at least once.

Eventually, they were led into a small chamber that had white painted walls, a cheery fire in a hearth that was almost art-deco in design, and a series of Edwardian drawing-room chairs around its edges. The cozy feel of the room was incongruous with the race of demons that had made it. They weren't known for having excellent—and refined—taste.

The chamber wasn't particularly large, so most of their

escort was forced to wait outside. Counting the wonderful antique chairs, though, there was probably enough space for the cloaked army to sit against the walls. Maybe that was a no-no, however. Only Speaker and two other demons followed them in, their cowls still firmly in place.

Were they afraid to show their faces? Or was there some kind of hierarchical structure that meant they had to keep hidden when in front of certain individuals?

She had no idea. But she probably should.

It wasn't like information on the Mortus was freely available, though, and Dru hadn't wanted to dig too deeply for fear they'd learn of her identity. People asking questions in the underworld generally raised eyebrows and got questions back in return. And because she didn't want to live in Inferno, enslaved to the Mortus, she had kept to herself. Even working as a blood-slave for Trick was a better alternative. At least she got to travel, that way.

But there might be a lover here you could have all for yourself...

Yeah, she doubted it.

From what she understood, Mortus females were bred with males to produce the optimum offspring. If they managed to find a mate among the available Mortus, they *might* be spared the attentions of other males. It depended on the status of the male.

That information had come directly from Trick, and she doubted he'd lie to her about it. Just cos he wanted to have sex with her, didn't mean that he devalued her mind; he knew that it was just as deadly a weapon as her claws, and if he pissed her off...

Sure, *she* couldn't kill her slave master, but that didn't mean she wasn't allowed to find someone who could.

No, having a lover wasn't worth being enslaved to any race, no matter that it might be nice.

Now is not the time to think about your lack of relationship status. Her life wasn't over yet, so there was no need to get maudlin.

She focused on the positives: they were standing in a warm room, Az was being quiet, and they weren't under immediate attack. She snuck a glance at the ring—the emerald was still dull. *But why did we end up here of all places?*

She needed some alone time with Az so she could see what the Hell he had been thinking. Literally *and* figuratively.

A heartbeat later, a door opened to their left and a man strode in the room. He wore no cloak, but had a circlet on his forehead, indicating he was some kind of big wig. *Probably a royal.* Not that she knew how the internal structure of the Mortus society worked, aside from men having all the power.

His long black hair was threaded with gray, giving him that silver-fox, George Clooney kind of appearance. He wore a suit more befitting the Victorian era, complete with a cravat, waistcoat and jacket, and his appearance was eerily similar to that of Speaker's.

They had to be related.

Wonderful. We were captured by some high-ranking Mortus, not just a flunky.

"What have you brought before me?" the new demon asked. He looked down his patrician nose at both of them, but his eyes lingered on her, making her feel like bugs were crawling over every square inch of her skin.

She didn't like this guy.

Not one bit.

"I found these two wandering in the forest while out on patrol."

"They are covered in blood."

"They claim to have been fighting Reynard's Imps."

Both of the royal guy's eyebrows rose. "There are no imps near our borders. They are only found in Sheol."

So father and son—uncle and nephew?—had stating the obvious in common, too.

"They claim to have teleported from there."

The older demon stepped forward, his nostrils flaring, and stopped a few feet in front of them. The two guards flanking them pressed closer, and Dru hissed as one bumped into her shoulder. "Touch me again and you'll lose the arm."

The backhand happened so quickly she didn't have time to block it. Blood burst in her mouth, and she raised a hand to her lip as she fought to control the pain. She stared at the royal—a slight smile danced around his mouth.

Oh, he'd *enjoyed* hurting her.

A low growl filled the room.

It was only when she felt the vibration against her arm that she realized it was coming from Az. His blue eyes had turned to chips of ice, his face brutal in its beauty as he glared at her attacker. His expression spoke of death.

Damn, that's hot, she thought, as she tongued the cut on the inside of her cheek. It was already healing, thankfully.

The head honcho spoke, "You will speak only when

spoken to, woman."

Oh, she *really* didn't like this guy.

With his obvious love of woman-beating, he had just gone to straight to number one on her private kill list; the guard who'd brushed up against her was ranked down near five-hundred or so. She didn't care that that the demon before them might be the leader of the entire Mortus clan. No one touched her.

Ever.

It took every bit of her self-control not to answer back, the slight tightening of Az's hand on her arm also warning her to keep quiet. She wasn't an idiot. She knew that if she spoke again now, a backhand to the face might be the least of her problems.

That didn't mean that she wasn't going to slice this bastard up into tiny, tiny pieces.

Just wait until Trick finds out. Not that he could do much, but if there was any upcoming contract that even hinted that a Mortus might be involved...

Death.

There would be so much death.

"Uncle, I believe the woman is of interest to us," Speaker said in smooth tones, cutting through Dru's fantasy.

Both of the assholes stared at her again.

This time, she let her anger show, felt it flow past her natural barriers, until her whole body pulsed with it. Her teeth clenched, and her back fought to bow. This was the unbridled hate-filled monster that lived in her veins. This was the creature that made her so deadly, despite the fact she was half-human.

This was what made her one of the best assassins in

the three realms.

The guard next to her stepped back, and the bastard before her blinked in surprise, his eyes narrowing, flickering with something akin to concern.

Az's arm stayed steady on hers, the mild tension in his muscles indicating he was alert but not alarmed. It helped her, his warmth and his relaxation. A deep breath, followed by another, and she was able to carefully wind back the monster, to encase it in the thin layers of her humanity.

This is what made her and Peony so different.

Peony's monster was close to her skin, to the point it affected her physical being, whereas Dru's was buried deep, but stronger. Nastier. It was her core, whereas Peony's inner self was human. It was probably why Dru had been sold into slavery, while Peony had been taken and raised in the Human Realm, by a woman who loved her.

Enough.

Now is not the time.

It *never* was the time. Self-pity was for the weak, and Dru was anything but weak.

"Take them to the cells," the demon said, flicking out a hand like they were nothing. "Let them think about their disrespect."

Our disrespect?

Oh boy.

This guy was gonna be so dead by the time she was through with him.

CHAPTER 16

They were escorted from the room with little fuss, although Azrael's eyes were drawn again and again to the purple bruise blooming on Dru's cheek. It looked painful, the spread of blue and violet marring her otherwise flawless skin. A growl fought to emerge once again.

That fucking Hell-scum bastard.

No, that was an insult to Hell-scum.

If this was how the Mortus demon ruled his people, no wonder Dru wasn't living among them. Then again, did they even realize what she was? Maybe they treated her poorly because she was a cambion.

Half-human was only half as good, according to a lot of demons.

He leaned closer to her and whispered, "You okay?"

She gave a tight nod, the black in her eyes finally dissipating until all that was left was the clear gray of her irises. But the subtle tension that radiated from her told him she wasn't happy with their situation.

Which was fine, because neither was he.

The asshole who looked like he was related to the crowned fucker—Mini Me, Azrael decided to call him— led them in a different circular route away from the drawing room. More ancient angelic text was scrawled on the walls of the tunnels, and he could make out small fragments here and there. Words like 'the' and 'and'. There were some commonalities between the ancient texts and the new, but not much.

It was too bad Raze wasn't the one being taken prisoner—that guy could read all kinds of ancient languages. In fact, he had so many crammed in his head he occasionally spoke the wrong one from time to time, or a pidgin version of something else. Before the burgeoning silver filaments in his wings had proclaimed him to be warrior class, he'd been in training to be a scholar. And then he'd spent centuries mastering warfare to join the Darts.

Azrael's gut clenched at the memories.

They'd all been so proud to fight for their race, elated to learn they were serving under Dina, who was a celebrated warrior so powerful that one day she might have even ascended to archangel status.

Of course, those rumors had been quashed quickly by the archangels themselves. Too much speculation was a bad thing, they'd said. *God's will is mysterious.*

Now, Azrael just thought they were hoarding the power for themselves. They didn't like the idea that a mere warrior could challenge the roles that had been handed down millennia ago by a now mostly-silent deity.

God's will was, after all, only spoken through the archangels. Nowadays, anyway.

Nice little system of power, there.

And yet, when he'd been in Heaven, he'd never questioned the structure. Had never doubted its righteousness, or his own. They were the good guys and they did good things. Angels weren't involved in petty squabbles, and power meant nothing to them.

Then Uriel had sliced off his wings. Had let them fall to the ground, had kicked them in front of him, so that they had been the only thing that filled Azrael's vision as the pain had threatened to destroy him.

It had been cruel, that last action.

The amputation hadn't been a lesson for Azrael, it had been a punishment, meant to frighten the masses of angels who would wonder how Heaven had been breached in the first place. In the end, it hadn't been about Azrael, or the Darts. It had been about consolidating the archangels' rule over Heaven.

So, even if he managed to return to Heaven, Azrael would never view things in the same way again. His innocence, his *trust*, had been destroyed along with the Inner Sanctum the day Heaven's Heart was stolen.

And he didn't think there was anything anyone could do to win it back.

Finding the damned artifact was a mission fraught with danger and doomed to failure. After all, Heaven had guarded only *one* piece of the Heart. No one had any idea where the other two fragments were.

"Pay attention," Dru murmured, bumping him gently with her hip.

He realized he'd lost track of his surrounds, and he was leaning more heavily on Dru than he probably needed to. Maybe he'd lost more blood than he'd thought.

They had travelled deeper into the cave system while he'd been daydreaming, the increasing humidity and the staleness of the air clues to their location. They were heading downward, into the depths of the bedrock that housed Inferno.

The ubiquitous cave systems kind of made sense, he thought.

Heaven was a world of air and clouds, light and softness. The Human Realm, in contrast, was of water, earth, air and fire. Tumultuous, rapidly changing, and vulnerable to alteration. And Hell, from the pieces he'd seen, were of the earth. Rocky, stable, and never-ending.

The Human Realm was a mix of the two extremes.

Perhaps that's why he'd grown to like it so much.

It was the gray area in between good and evil—much like himself.

Minutes later, they came to another sloping corridor, this one terminating in a huge door with all kinds of script engraved onto its stone surface. And it was clearly spelled: the glow of magic hurt his eyes in the darkened underground.

We aren't going to break out of here easily, even if we could remember our way back.

Muttering something arcane-sounding, Mini-Me pushed on the door, which opened with a whoosh and a rush of long-undisturbed air. He turned and nodded to the soldiers on either side of them, who shoved at Azrael and Dru, indicating they should lead the way. Azrael wanted to push them in return, but controlled the urge. It would only lead to more injuries Dru and he could ill afford.

Once through the doorway, the panel swung back into

place with a whisper.

Darkness.

Then, one by one, torches sprang to life along the walls, lighting a small antechamber with a disused guard desk carved entirely from stone.

Mini-Me shoved his way past them, careful not to let the bare skin of his hands come into contact with their bodies.

The guards wore gloves. Was there a reason why Mini-Me could walk around gloveless, when they couldn't?

Maybe Dru would be able to tell him.

No angelic text here, Azrael realized, staring at the walls. Instead, they were inscribed in a series of demonish languages. Raze would just about ejaculate from excitement if he were locked in here with nothing more than a notepad.

Different priorities.

And different fantasies.

Another shove against their backs, and he and Dru were herded toward another door, this one pure metal, and gleaming with more magical inscriptions. Mini-Me laid a palm against the portal, muttered a few words in a language Azrael had never before heard, and then they were walking through the doorway, into a short corridor lined with steel-barred cells. There were no torches, but the bars pulsed with magic, so that they lit the room in staccato bursts.

There were only ten cells.

Doesn't seem like the Mortus ordinarily keep prisoners.

He didn't know if that was a good thing, or a bad thing. He'd hold off on judgment. See what the food was like, what the service offered…

He could almost hear Dina's voice in his head telling him to be less flippant. He guessed some things hadn't changed.

He just hoped that she was still alive to call him on his attitude once again.

"Should we split them up, my lord?" the guard closest to Dru asked.

Mini-Me spun on his heel, his cold stare taking them in. "May as well put them next to each other. They'll be able to speak unless we gag them, so separating them won't make too much of a difference. Plus, there's spells in place that will prevent them from teleporting. Take their packs, though."

From the gleam in the bastard's eyes, he was contemplating hog-tying and gagging them anyway, just for kicks.

A few moments later, Dru and Azrael were hustled into their cells, minus any bindings and their backpacks. Azrael felt the loss of his pack keenly—no extra magic, no extra weapons…His cell was closest to the door, and hers was the next one down. The guards slammed the doors home, locked them, and left.

Mini-Me stood in the corridor, in front of Dru's cell. His hands were clasped behind his back, and the bastard almost looked relaxed. But his eyes were covetous as they took in Dru's form. Azrael didn't like the expression one bit.

"My uncle will call upon you both when he's made a decision as to what to do with you. Until then." The door swung closed behind him, leaving them alone in the dungeon.

A bluish glow pulsed from the spelled bars, the irregular lighting making Dru's bruise appear even more livid.

"No threats? No warnings?" Azrael mused.

How over-confident were these assholes, that they'd left their weapons on them?

Dru shot him a bemused look, then walked over to the rear wall of her cell. She sat down on the stone floor, close to the bars that separated their new homes. She looked small, alone in her corner of space. "No need to."

He limped over and lowered himself carefully to the floor next to her on his side of the bars. He leaned against the warded steel, which grew warmer, but did nothing else sinister. She did the same thing from her side, so they were sort-of touching.

"Why doesn't he need to make threats?" Azrael asked.

"They're the Mortus. We're only here for their entertainment. Once they grow tired of us, we're dead. They don't need to use threats to get that message across."

"I didn't hear anything about dying."

"They are the direct descendants of Satan. Their general attitude to outsiders is clear." She sighed and leaned the non-bruised side of her face against the bars.

"Does it hurt much?" he asked, turning his head a little so his lips briefly brushed against the side of her head.

"I've had worse. It was more the surprise that got me."

He didn't like that she'd suffered previously, but she *was* a fighter. It was rare you could be in their profession and have no war-wounds to speak of. And that backhand *had* been uncalled for. It was like the bastard had just wanted to hear the sting of his gloved hand against her flesh.

"Do you think they can hear us?"

"They've probably got listening spells in place."

They were silent for a few moments, then Dru asked, "How's your leg?"

"Healing." Slower than he'd like, but then he probably still had the remnants of her toxin flowing through his veins. The others had said he'd be a bit weaker than normal for a while. It's why Yael had volunteered for this mission.

He probably would be done and dusted by now, too.

The jerk.

Yael wouldn't have stopped to help Dru and gotten himself trapped by that damned sorcerer. He would've probably already found the Orb and be using it right now to find the first piece of Heaven's Heart.

The thing was though, Azrael didn't regret his decision.

Not one bit.

CHAPTER 17

"Why didn't you just kill them in the forest?" Uncle Alvin asked. "They were clearly trespassing."

They were seated in the council chambers, the other members of the ruling council uninvited to their little meeting. They'd phrased their catch-up as an uncle-nephew get-together, although Godric was sure the others were suspicious as to why they'd been excluded, especially since he'd brought home two prisoners and then locked them up in the dungeon, rather than kill them.

Them's the breaks.

Godric didn't particularly care for the council and their delicate sensibilities, at least, not right now. He had bigger fish to fry—like getting his uncle taken care of. But that was an issue for another century. He had time. After all, that was about the only thing the Mortus had: endless boring existence.

He spread his hands over the smooth surface of the large oval table that dominated the room. The empty chairs looked a little lonely. Oh well. Not his problem.

The tabletop in front of them was covered in delicate fruits and spiced meats for their pleasure.

What a waste. His uncle would take but a few mouthfuls of the feast, and Godric wasn't allowed to eat more than his elder without causing an etiquette scandal. And he was starving.

He'd been on patrol for the past week straight, and had been returning to the enclave when they'd spotted the intruders. He'd been fantasizing about a juicy mystery-meat steak and about six pitchers of ale when he'd noticed the newcomers. It had been a lucky find, and one he wasn't about to highlight to his uncle. The man was bad-tempered enough as it was.

Then again, having to rule a bunch of cretins like the Mortus would do that to a guy.

Alvin Mercan might technically be the king of the Mortus, but he still had to answer to the ruling council, who were pains in his royal highness' ass. He wasn't as autonomous as he liked to tell himself, and Godric knew it. Just like he knew that, as the only male heir, he had a lot more leeway than the average high-ranking lordling.

Even if, according to his uncle, his blood *was* tainted.

But with a dwindling number of female Mortus demons, it only made sense for their kind to search for mates outside their species. Both Godric's father and his other uncle had done so. And apparently both had been successful.

Although, that did depend on your definition of 'success'.

Godric popped a loganberry in his mouth, shutting his eyes briefly at the explosion of sweet juice as he bit through its skin. "Did you have a good look at the woman before you damaged her?" He should have probably added 'Your Majesty' to the end of that sentence, but if Alvin wanted a blood-related male heir, then he'd take what he could get.

Alvin snorted. "It was a mere tap."

Godric stared; that didn't answer the question. "But did you *look* at her?"

His uncle rolled his eyes. "She was nothing more than a human cambion. What concern is she to us? Just kill them and be done with it. I don't know why we need to talk about it. I do enough talking as it is with those meatheads." He nodded at the vacant chairs.

Godric inhaled, drawing on his considerable well of patience—something he'd inherited from his mother, he figured. "She looks like Uncle Clement."

Clement—the younger brother of Alvin and of Godric's father.

The king choked on a slice of kiwi fruit. "*What?*"

If you ignored the odd skin color, and the white hair… "She is, in fact, his spitting image, albeit a mere female."

And she was quite pretty, although he'd keep that opinion to himself.

"My brother is dead. He had no legitimate offspring."

"I didn't say she was his *legitimate* offspring," Godric murmured.

His uncle sat back in his chair. "If she is his child, she is an abomination."

"She is half-Mortus demon," Godric said. "Can we afford to be so fussy?"

Especially since the women they had were beginning to tire of endless copulation and being used as broodmares. Even the harsh punishments his uncle forced on them were not enough to quell their rising ire.

"You have no proof she is Clement's offspring."

"We can get proof, if you need it." But Godric had heard the rumors over the years—about a cambion assassin who could kill a man with a scratch of her nails. Considered one of the deadliest paid-killers on the market, she worked for some guild based out of Tartarus.

He'd never investigated her before, because he'd never thought that she could be Mortus. And he had looked for others of their kind, knowing that Uncle Clement had left to spread his wild oats among the demon population. Uncle Alvin thought any such offspring was beneath the Mortus, but because Godric was a result of a similar union, he wasn't quite so fussy.

And he played a long game.

The Mortus culture was stagnating and they needed fresh blood. He didn't know for sure if the assassin and the cambion in his uncle's dungeon were the same woman, but she had a guild logo on her shirt, and she was a halfbreed.

If she *wasn't* the assassin, all the better; they could just keep her, because if she was truly part Mortus, then extracting her from her guild was of the highest priority.

And the guilds didn't tend to let their killers go without a hefty price. And a lot of death.

"Get me this proof and I might consider adding her to the harem," Uncle Alvin said, then popped a grape into his mouth.

The harem: the stable of women used for breeding purposes by any upper-ranking lord of the Mortus. Adding a possible assassin when there was already palpable agitation in the harem was only going to end in disaster.

But Godric had to tackle one problem at a time.

"I'll get the proof."

"What of the male?" Alvin asked.

"I am not sure what he is. But I get a strange vibe of *goodness* from him." The very word tasted bad. He wasn't used to dealing with people who didn't have the same streak of evil running through their veins. Even his mother's race, the Alaris, who were largely peaceable, had a dark streak a mile wide. It was in their nature.

Kindness of heart was just...wrong.

"Give me the proof about the girl, and then we'll kill the male publicly. If she is Mortus, that will teach her for straying from her roots."

Godric liked the idea of ending the male, but he had the feeling it would just make the cambion angrier.

Which, for some reason, had him worried.

She's only half-Mortus. How bad can she be?

CHAPTER 18

The throbbing in Dru's cheek had turned into a dull ache, so much so that she wondered if it was already well underway toward being fixed. She didn't normally heal so quickly, but maybe being within her home realm changed things. Gave her some extra dark mojo or something.

I don't really want to think of this place as home.

She shut her eyes against the strobing caused by the numerous spells warding the prison. In a way, maybe she *had* been lucky that the demon nurse who had delivered her had decided to sell her on the black market. If that bitch demon had given her to the Mortus, Dru would have been nothing more than a broodmare for her entire life. *If* they'd wanted to taint their genes with hers.

She was more likely to have been drowned as a baby for merely existing.

Az's deep voice cut through her thoughts. "So, explain to me more about the Mortus. We were only taught they were the bad guys who were toxic to touch. Like, really bad guys. Satan's-get bad."

She didn't like that she enjoyed hearing him speak. But he'd supported her throughout their ordeal here, and that made her happy…She was probably going to be in for a world of hurt when everything was done and dusted, no matter how it turned out.

Because she actually *liked* him.

"You probably know more about them than I do," Dru admitted.

He turned to face her. "How is that possible?"

Dayum, he's hot. Even with the crazy pulsed light turning his bronzed skin a weird silvery color.

"I didn't grow up with them, and they're renowned for being secretive."

"Thank God that you got away from their style of upbringing."

She shot him a look.

"What? I'm still an angel," he said. "And these guys are assholes of the highest order. I can only imagine their attitudes to raising children. Probably pedophiles, the lot of them."

"I won't argue with you on child-raising point." Although his last claim made her feel sick. Dru had done a lot of bad things in her life, and didn't regret all that many of them, if she was honest. But touching kids? No. She'd cut the hands and genitals off anybody who thought that was a good pastime.

And that dude with the crown, who hit her just for talking? He was probably depraved enough that he'd try just about anything.

Pure evil was pure evil, after all.

She still wanted to slice him up into tiny pieces and feed him to a bunch of Reynard's Imps. That way they could shit him out afterward, and he'd be forever known as just that—crap some demon excreted.

Maybe she'd start doing that with all of her kills. It'd be a tidy way to hide the evidence. And now she knew where a bunch of those bastard imps liked to hunt...

"Hello?" Az brushed a hand down her arm. She fought the urge to snatch her limb away, her normal reaction to any kind of touch. But the contact felt nice, soothing. Right.

I deserve nice things.

And for the first time ever, she kind of believed that. Peony wasn't the only one worthy of pleasant stuff.

I just have to get out of here, get that stupid Orb, and make a few other kills, then I'll be free. I'll buy Peony's freedom and we can leave Hell, find somewhere new to live. She can be a doctor, and I'll do something.

"Hello?" He touched her again.

"Sorry, was thinking about how I am going to dispose of that crowned-fucker's body once I kill him."

"Ohhh, do tell."

"No, you'll steal my idea. It's that good."

"Spoilsport."

"You betcha." It was strange, how their banter had become...fun.

"So, how come you weren't born here?" Az asked.

Dru's breath seized for a moment. This was a topic she'd prefer *not* to talk about. But—

Maybe it will hurt less if I tell someone...

The thought almost sealed her lips forever. She was over the trauma of discovering she'd been sold as a baby while her identical twin sister had been kept and raised in a loving home. She really was.

The fact you need to tell yourself that—

"My mother was human," Dru began.

"I got that bit," Az said with a slight smirk.

She pinched his arm.

"Ow."

"Shut up and let me talk."

He rubbed his bicep. "Be my guest."

"My mother was human and my father was Mortus. I guess they must have been mates—otherwise, I don't know how she survived bedding him." That was something she had not speculated on in any great detail, because *gross.* However, only mates—and apparently angels—were exempt from the Mortus toxin. "She gave birth in a hospital largely staffed by demons. From what I've been able to piece together, once it was known we were twins, one of the nurses decided to sell one of us to make some cash."

"There are *two* of you? Wait, what did your mother do about that?"

"She didn't do anything. She didn't know she had twins."

"How could she not know *that?*"

"We were born by C-section." She'd been able to find that out from the medical records, although the rest of the file had been excised, covered up in a staggering case of malpractice.

"So, one of the nurses realized you were cambion and sold you?"

"As far as I can tell. The second nurse kept my twin with my mother." And then her mother had died of complications—bled out. Whether or not there had been deliberate mismanagement of her procedure... *that* Dru had never been able to find out.

"What happened to your twin?"

"When the other nurse realized our mother was dead, she took my sister. They recorded that all three of us had died."

"Your sister was sold, too?"

"No, the nurse kept and raised her as her own."

Az let out a low whistle. "You never knew her growing up?"

Dru shook her head, tired to her bones. A small lump had formed in the back of her throat. "No, we had very different upbringings."

"You were both raised in Tartarus?"

"No, I was raised by a guild that sells orphans into blood-slavery. When it became clear I had a natural talent for killing…"

"You were then sold to an assassin guild as a child?"

"Correct."

"Where was your sister raised?"

"The Human Realm."

"How did you find out about her?"

"My current boss humored me when I said I wanted to find out what had happened to my birth mother. I managed to track down the nurses who delivered us…"

She had been prepared to make an exception to her 'mostly professional kills' rule for the two nurses who'd destroyed her life. The first had died rather painfully. The Silask demon had been screaming that she was sorry the entire time, that she'd needed the money to feed her litter. But that hadn't been enough, not when Dru already knew the woman had a habit of stealing infants and living off the profits—and that the demon had never had any children of her own.

"Let me guess," Az said. "They're dead."

"Only one of them. My sister was well-looked after. I let her abductor live." In truth, the encounter with Peony's adopted mother—Selene—hadn't gone well, but the woman had survived it mostly because Peony had come home and interrupted them.

Peony had had a fucking ideal life, except for her little quirk, and the nurse who'd taken her *had* loved her. She'd worked hard to send Peony to medical school, given her a home and a family. If she hadn't, Peony would probably have ended up much like Dru.

Dru hadn't been happy about it at the time, but Peony had been right to stop her killing Selene. Now the damned nurse sent her Christmas cards.

That's where Peony gets it from. That…kindness.

"What happened to your father?"

She played with the dull emerald ring. "That, I have no idea about." Even Trick hadn't been able to learn anything. The bastard had promised to 'investigate the issue', but Dru did wonder how hard he'd looked. Sometimes birth parents could negate the blood-contracts, and her boss might not have wanted to risk that. Then again, Dru was often more trouble than she was worth (Trick's words), so maybe he had actually put some effort into it.

"Perhaps these guys know," Az said slowly.

"They might." But she wasn't about to ask.

The door swung open, and Speaker strode into the cells like he owned them. He probably did, especially considering his resemblance to the fist-wielding jerk with the coronet.

Speaker glanced over at them, giving them a small smirk. "It's time."

CHAPTER 19

The demon with the gentle hands was back.

Her cart rattled into the cell, and he turned his head away from the door so she wouldn't know he had been watching and waiting for her arrival. How pathetic was he, that he craved the company of a creature he had once been sworn to kill on sight?

He was still sworn to do so, he supposed. After all, he hadn't been kicked out of Heaven, he had been abducted. Did that even make him fallen?

Zadkiel—no, he told himself. He was Z now—had spent many long hours agonizing over that very thought. Would his fellow Darts really want to save someone who had disgraced his kind as much as he had? After all, both he and Dina had been taken by surprise. He'd been blinded early into the attack, so he didn't know the names of his attackers or how they'd even gotten into Heaven.

That lack of knowledge ate at him, even as his vision had returned; the loss of Dina burned him day and night.

She wasn't here, and the little demon healer didn't know of another angel being held in the same prison complex. He could still sense when a person lied to him—maybe he wasn't entirely fallen, after all—so he knew she was telling the truth.

So where is Dina?

His captors hadn't wanted to keep him, he remembered that much. He was a risk, they'd said. And so they'd eventually sold him into slavery, after plucking his wings and torturing him for fun. Here he'd stayed ever since, only to be visited by the little healer, or by his new 'employer'.

Trick.

Everything about that man was a lie. Whenever the guild leader stood in the cell, Z's teeth ached with the force of the untruths that swirled around him.

"How are you today?" the demon healer asked. Her voice was low and soothing, and she smelled like baking spices and sugar.

Z wanted to tell her to leave him so he could die in peace, but kindness was a rare thing in the world, so he'd come to learn. And he appreciated whatever she could give him, an object of pity though that made him.

She tsked at his silence. "On the floor again, I see."

Every time she came in, she seemed annoyed to find him there. The healer appeared to think he was better off on the lumpy bedding, even though it scrunched his dying wings. He could tell her it hurt him to lie on the bed, but she obviously had her own ideas about how he should be healing.

And how he wasn't.

She picked him up with a grunt before depositing him on the bedding once more, this time on his stomach. She never touched him skin-to-skin, a sensation he was beginning to crave; just to feel another's warmth, to know he wasn't so alone. But she always wore gloves and was covered neck-to-toe in what appeared to be human hospital scrubs.

"I will give your wings a wash."

She didn't seem to mind that he didn't answer. He was too busy bracing himself for the pain.

He was worried about his wings. They were rotting, the flesh falling away from his bones, no matter the care the demon woman gave him. How long before they were gone entirely?

She gently patted at the wilted wings, and he fought the urge to scream. The pain wasn't as bad as his frustration; he almost yelled that she should just cut the things off and be done with it. What was the point in all this cleaning and jabbing and bandaging when it clearly wasn't working?

"Oh."

Her soft murmur of surprise sliced through his thoughts. Without thinking, he muttered, "What?"

"Your wings." Her voice was full of wonder.

He turned to look at her properly. Her near-white hair was tied back in a no-nonsense bun, and her honey-colored skin was warm, inviting. But it was her gray eyes, and their inherent sweetness that locked his attention.

"What about them?" He barely recognized his own voice, so rough and raw was it.

"You have new feathers."

"What?" He struggled to sit up, to look, but she pressed both gloved hands against his shoulders, pushing him back against the horrid lumpy mattress.

"You will injure yourself," she said. "They are just pin

feathers, but they are new." A smile bloomed on her face, turning her from pretty to breathtaking. "I knew we were doing the right thing."

She hurried back to her cart and gathered more supplies.

He lay there, stunned by the news of his wings, but more stunned by his reaction to *her*.

This *attraction* wasn't real, he told himself. It was what the humans called Stockholm Syndrome or something like it. She was his captor as much as Trick was. Z was just susceptible because he'd been tortured, kidnapped and poisoned. That was it.

She was moving his wings around now, murmuring to herself the whole while, but he wasn't listening, trapped inside his mind with his growing panic.

Any person who was kind to him, he'd appreciate them. Yes, that was it. Appreciation. He was grateful to her for her kindness. It was not *attraction*.

You're delusional, he told himself. As if he could ever be attracted to a *demon*. Most angels didn't even experience desire, anyway. Sure, they experimented, as Dina had experimented with him from time to time. But he didn't feel *lust* for the healer.

No.

That was just absurd.

Nonetheless, he couldn't deny that she had helped him: his wings were growing back. Now he just had to get stronger, so that when—not *if*—the Darts came for him, he'd be ready.

The healer gave him a triumphant grin. "Okay, now, let's try and get some broth into you."

CHAPTER 20

They had been tied to two chairs, back-to-back, so Azrael couldn't see Dru's face. Ropes were looped around their torsos and their hands tied behind their backs, although their legs were free. No one had been stupid enough to walk within kicking distance.

Yet.

He was keeping an eye out.

They hadn't been taken to the same room as before—now they were in a small hall of sorts, where the intricately carved walls were lined with expensively dressed green-skinned demons and guards in hooded capes. The clothing on the courtiers appeared to have been fashionable two centuries ago, at least according to what Azrael had seen on TV. He wasn't sure if this was a result of their being isolated from the rest of Hell, or the Mortus realm not getting mainstream media access.

Observing the crowd, Azrael decided that cloaks must be part of the standard soldier uniform. Maybe they wore them so that if they encountered strangers, they wouldn't poison them by accident?

As he counted the guards in his line of vision, he raised an eyebrow. There were at least fifteen, with about ten of them hovering around a small group of female Mortus. The women wore dresses complete with corsets, and far too much lace for anyone's sanity. They were generally pretty, he noted, despite the greenish skin, but none had gray eyes like Dru, nor did they boast the fire that roared within her like a beacon.

Turning his attention back to the guards, he wondered if there were the same number in the other half of the room; if so, thirty men had been posted for this little meet-and-greet. Not that he and Dru would be able to manage an effective escape right now, tied up as they were.

There.

His and Dru's packs sat on a raised dais to his right. The packs were open, with his and Dru's weapons carelessly discarded on the nearby floor. *They went through our stuff.*

He wondered what they had stolen.

He'd worry about that later. At least the delay between being shoved in the cells and being herded back up here had resulted in his calf healing almost completely. He couldn't really capitalize on that right now, but he was planning.

He was really getting sick of the shitty odds.

The bastard with the coronet strode into the room from Azrael's right, nodding at the bystanders. He wore a purple cape and a newer, even more fancy crown.

The guards lowered their hoods.

Interesting.

Most of the males had dark hair, in shades of black,

gray and brown. Not a single blond to be seen.

Dru must have gotten her coloring from her human mother.

The head honcho indicated the guy who'd discovered them in the forest. "Prince Godric has called us here today to investigate why our lands were trespassed upon by these…individuals."

Prince Godric?

Joy for them, they'd been captured by royalty.

Where had all his luck gone? That's what Azrael wanted to know.

It disappeared the same day your wings did.

Ouch. Even his conscience was turning out to be an asshole.

"Your Majesty, thank you." That cold-eyed bastard Godric stepped forward, his gaze raking the courtiers and guards, a slight curl to his upper lip, like he thought he was better than everyone here. His cloak was gone, and he was dressed in something a little more fashionable, but still way over the top.

Tuxedos are so not necessary.

"I have a few questions for the woman first." He moved toward Dru.

Azrael tested his bindings, but they'd been tied well; there wasn't any real give in the ropes. *Damn it.*

"What species of cambion are you?" Godric asked, his voice raised so that it filled the chamber.

Murmurs roiled through the crowd at the word 'cambion'. Like Dru was diseased or something.

Bastards.

Her voice rang out, challenging. "You mean you can't tell?"

Fuck, he was proud of her. He couldn't see her

expression, but he reckoned it was pure sarcasm and ice.

The king glared in Dru's direction, but Godric just appeared amused. Like this was all a game to him. And who knew? It probably was. Evil beings found entertainment in the strangest scenarios.

"My theory is you are half-Mortus, but this has been met with some resistance."

"Why? Because Mortus demons wouldn't ever fuck a human?"

The king strode closer to Dru. "Your disrespect is wearing on my patience."

"Well, I'm half-human. Guess you can't help genetics."

Azrael smirked. From the stunned looks on the courtiers' faces, they weren't used to a woman speaking her mind. *Or even speaking, probably.*

Godric moved closer. "You admit that you are half-Mortus?"

She hadn't admitted anything, actually, but Azrael felt her shrug. "Appears that way."

"Do you know the name of your Mortus parent?"

"No."

"Was it your mother or father?"

From the way the women were clustered together on the edges of the room, and how the guards hovered near them, Azrael had the feeling this was a pointless question. As if they'd ever let a woman leave by herself.

"Father."

"Do you have his name?"

"No, I just said that."

The king's voice cut through the questioning. "Then how can we know she is Mortus?"

A small smile from Godric, making his eyes gleam with malice. "Why don't we test her?"

"Good point." The king turned to face the people behind Azrael. "Lord Farcon!"

"Your Majesty?"

"Please   complete   a   preliminary   test   on the...cambion."

"With pleasure."

The sounds of rustling, and then Azrael felt the warmth of Dru's back vanish. She'd been untied. He turned his head to see she had been herded toward the king by two guards on either side of her. He exhaled. She was fine. Her eyes were flashing, and her hands were still fastened behind her back, but she appeared well enough, given their circumstances.

Thank God.

A   male   Mortus   demon—Farcon,   presumably— approached Dru, his fussy purple and green striped suit-and-cravat combination eye-wateringly bad. He pulled a glove off his hand, one finger at a time, his expression one of smug contentment.

Way to drag it out.

But from the silence in the room, the others were lapping up the drama. *Guess they don't get out much.*

Lord Farcon handed the glove to a nearby guard, who took it with a bemused look, then glanced around, as if wondering where to place it. He decided to hold on to it, tucking it into the folds of his cloak.

Farcon closed the distance between himself and Dru, stopping a mere foot away. She tilted her head back, chin raised in defiance. A dark gleam entered the Mortus demon's eyes, like he relished this resistance, but not for the right reasons. The way the man's still-gloved hand opened and closed in a fist made Azrael think Farcon would love nothing more than to beat Dru's rebellion out of her.

Finally, the lord leaned forward and whispered something in Dru's ear, before running a caressing finger down her cheek. The crowd inhaled as one. She hissed, her eyes turning completely black, her hands clenching behind her back.

Azrael wrenched at his restraints, but it was no good. The rough rope rubbed his skin raw, and his blood was making everything slick. Soon, his wrists just slid around uselessly in the bindings.

The crowd stared at the tableau before them: Dru ramrod straight, Farcon almost twitching with excitement. Even the bastard with the crown was rapt.

Azrael waited. One heartbeat. Two.

But Dru remained upright, her lip curling slightly in contempt.

Azrael let out a breath he hadn't realized he'd been holding.

Suddenly, the rope around his wrists gave way, as if it had simply dissolved.

What? He frowned in confusion. But he wasn't about to reject his surprising good fortune. Rather than leap up and attack, however, he kept his arms behind his back, waiting to see how this played out.

Plus, he was still tied to the chair with rope around his chest.

Dru's eyes remained inky pools of darkness, but a small, twisted smile played at her lips. She shook her head, and the bindings around her wrists dropped to the floor. "Is that all you've got?"

Everything happened quickly after that.

CHAPTER 21

The ropes around Dru's wrists hit the floor behind her in a slithery mess.

Finally.

She increased her smirk, just to see the fire flash in Lord Fart-on's eyes. Right before he'd trailed his finger down her cheek, he'd whispered "I can't wait to see you writhe in pain." Then he'd leered at her, like it would be the best turn-on he'd ever had.

Well, maybe it would be.

The thing was, Dru couldn't wait to see *him* screaming in agony.

She remembered the cold contact of his toxin with her cheek, her initial panic that maybe, maybe because she was a cambion, she'd be less tolerant of their race's poison…But there'd been no pain, no discomfort—although he'd wanted there to be. At the least, he'd hoped she would hurt; at best, he probably would have enjoyed watching her die.

She lashed out with a clawed hand, raking a trail of blood down the Mortus demon's cheek.

"You bitch!" The lord's hand rose automatically to his wounds as gasps and yells sounded. He made to strike her, but his arm dropped uselessly to his side, his eyes wide with horror.

The nearest guard took a step closer, but paused when Dru dropped into a fighting stance, loose-limbed and ready for anything. She wiggled her now-clawed fingers in a 'come and get it' gesture. Her claws were her best weapon; the Mortus demons' reliance on their own toxin as a major deterrent would be their undoing, and the guard seemed to realize that.

Within seconds of her attack, Lord Fart-on's eyes rolled back in his head, and he *howled*. The tortured sound rose through the room, until Dru saw the few Mortus females present cupping their hands over their ears.

The demon collapsed to the floor, convulsing, bloody foam frothing at his mouth, limbs flailing uselessly.

No one stepped forward to help him.

A few heartbeats later, he stopped moving.

Dead.

Dru would put good money on that.

"He's fainted," the nearest guard said.

Angry shouts arose around the room, but Dru tuned them out. She needed to be ready for an attack, not a streak of profanity.

"Check his pulse." Godric nodded at the body.

"I would use gloves." Dru began flicking Lord Fart's skin out from under her claws, her disrespect clear.

"Gloves?" Godric gave her a sharp glance.

"Just a precaution." She shot him an oily smile.

The guard withdrew Lord Fart's glove from his cloak and slipped it on his hand. There was a sense of irony in there, somewhere. Considering the pain the toxin caused, it *was* possible the guy could have just fainted. Being a full Mortus demon, he should have been immune to Dru's toxin, but she'd never tested hers against theirs before.

And, well, cambions didn't play by genetic rules. It was part of why they were so hated—things went *wrong* when humans bred with demons.

"By Satan's holy balls—" the king barked.

The guard kneeled down and felt for Lord Fart's pulse. A hush descended, as if that would help the demon feel whether or not the noble was dead.

After a few moments, he shook his head.

Godric frowned, snatched on a glove, and then checked for a pulse himself, as if he couldn't believe the result. He stood slowly, shaking his head. "Lord Farcon is dead."

A wail sounded through the room, and then shouts. The king held up his hands, then pointed at Dru. "You will pay for this."

How…cliched.

She shrugged and twisted the dull emerald ring on her finger. *Hurry up and glow.* "I thought it only fair that I test him in return. There was no point in it being a one-sided experiment."

"*You*—" Godric spluttered, expression filled with disbelief.

"I survived his toxin. But there was no guarantee *he* would survive *mine*."

"You are nothing but a cambion!" the king shouted.

She prodded the body with a toe. At least Lord Fart hadn't vacated his bladder and bowels yet. Death wasn't pretty; she should know. "True. But it seems like my poison is stronger than yours. Well, stronger than *his*."

Dru had often wondered if her being cambion could have made her more potent, deadlier, but she'd never had any reason to put it to the test. She'd also been concerned that the opposite could be true—that she wouldn't survive meeting another of her kind. She barely even touched Peony, whose skin was more like a typical Mortus demon's. Although, that was more because Peony was paranoid *everyone* who came into contact with her without protection would die.

And, well, Dru hadn't lived her entire life as a slave to croak it before she'd tasted freedom.

The king nodded at the body. "Remove Lord Farcon and take the prisoners back to the holding cells." More guards stepped forward, all wearing gloves. Two bent down and picked up the body, while two more went for Dru and Az.

"I demand justice!" Another demon stepped forward, his face eerily similar to that of the dead Lord Fart.

"Justice?" Godric echoed, like the idea was a foreign one.

Maybe it is. These guys are relatives of Satan, after all. And the first ruler of Hell wasn't known for his forgiving nature.

"She killed my brother! She deserves to be punished."

"And what kind of punishment do you propose?" Godric's voice flowed smoothly over the crowd, his tone too even, too cold to be taken as anything other than a promise of death.

Too bad the other guy didn't seem to realize that.

"She should be beaten and fucked until she is

comatose, kept alive only to provide offspring."

Rapists. They are a bunch of rapists.

Well, this guy and his brother were, and she figured the attitude would be echoed across most of the male Mortus in the room, from the way they were nodding.

Fuckers.

She was rapidly changing her opinion on pro bono work, because slicing this guy's throat open was growing more appealing by the second.

"There's a slight problem with your plan," Dru said.

"No one asked you, *whore.*" He spat on the floor.

Ewww.

There was no excuse for spitting, not inside. Even she, who'd been raised in a goddamn orphanage, knew better than that.

"Oh no, your name-calling has hurt my feelings." She pouted.

The king looked at her like she'd lost her mind. And maybe she had. Then again, maybe the Mortus weren't used to women speaking up.

"And what would that problem be?" Godric asked, seeming to have grown bored with Lord Fart's relative.

"Don't humor her!" the rapist shouted.

Godric's spine turned to steel, his expression hardening into a cold mask. Well, cold*er*.

"Did you just raise your voice to a member of the royal family?" The king's eyes turned flinty as both he and Godric stared at the dead demon's relative.

"She is an abomination. You cannot allow her to talk in such a way. She will poison the mind of the females present."

Poison the minds..? The females who, in Dru's

peripheral vision, seemed to shrink in on themselves in an effort to become less noticeable? Yeah, her talking back was going to cause a full-scale rebellion. She could see it now.

Oh, she wanted to puke it was so disgusting. They may as well put a sign at their lair's entrance: 'misogynists only'.

"I asked her a question." Godric flicked something from his sleeve. "Are you telling me that she should ignore a question from *her prince*?"

Godric wasn't her prince. Not at all. But since he was currently on her side, she'd roll with it.

Finally, it appeared to sink home that the idiot was in trouble. "N-n-no."

Glancing quickly at Az, she could see he was doing something with his hands behind his back. Had he managed to partially free himself? If so, they were going to party. Big time.

"So," Godric turned back to her. She snapped her attention back to the demon. "What is your problem with Orphel's punishment?"

Oh, like the fact it had been a totally unreasonable request?

"Well, it's not just my claws that are poisonous." She held her palms out.

"Your skin did not affect Lord Farcon."

"My skin isn't toxic."

"Then what is the issue?"

"My...uh..." How to say this in public without humiliating herself in front of Az? There probably wasn't a way, but she wasn't about to be used for a broodmare. *Ever.* "...lady parts are toxic."

"Your *what*?"

"My lady parts. Vagina. Magical hoo-hoo. Va-jay-jay. You know."

Az flinched in her peripheral vision, and she thought he might have muttered something like, "Nice to know". She couldn't be sure.

"You expect us to believe your womanly attributes are poisonous?" Godric was frowning now.

She snorted. *'Womanly attributes'.*

"You could try and ask my ex-lovers, but they all died so quickly…" Which was partially why she'd settled on a no-touching policy. Watching a guy die—painfully—after trying to get past third base had been a little soul-destroying, and she wasn't into self-pity. Or guilt.

"Kill her!" Lord Fart's brother shouted.

The king turned his flinty stare from the demon to Dru. "If she can't be used to breed…"

"You assume she's telling the truth," Godric mused.

"Why would I lie about something so embarrassing?" she replied.

The king nodded his head. "Why, indeed."

Whatever that meant.

"There are human methods of conception we could try…" Godric murmured to the king, probably not intending for her to overhear. But she was only a few feet away and her ears worked fine.

Hell no.

She was not going to be used as a fucking lab experiment to help swell the Mortus demons' ranks.

Spinning around, she slashed out with her claws, cutting through the bindings around Az's chest. He sprang to his feet, wrists covered in blood. She winced in sympathy. That would have hurt.

"Show time," Az murmured, disabling a guard in the blink of an eye, and snatching a knife from the fallen soldier.

The guards leaped into action, circling them. Dru looked over one of their broad shoulders, meeting Godric's gaze, then the king's. "How many of these men have to die before you let us go?"

"You will die before you leave," the king declared.

Yeah, we'll see about that.

She didn't believe in being overly confident, but she had an advantage over the Mortus that even she couldn't have predicted. *She* was deadly to *them*.

If they got within claw-distance…

Az grunted next to her, and then suddenly a body was flying right past her, blood spraying from a sliced neck, splashing her with hot drops.

One of the cloaked guards stepped forward, sword extended, but Dru neatly sidestepped and raked a single claw down the side of his neck. The answering scream nearly pierced her eardrum.

"Sorry," she murmured.

So not sorry.

A green glow caught her attention. *Finally.*

Moving back, she grabbed Az's arm, while twisting the ring with her thumb.

There's no place like home.

Nothing happened.

More guards closed in. They were wary now, some still with one eye on their twitching comrade. Horror was stamped on almost every face she could see, but it was slowly morphing into rage, the room mutating into a furnace of hatred.

Her heartbeat accelerated, and she tried the ring again. Again, they failed to teleport to her room in the Halcyon Guild.

Fuck.

A guard was within range now; she swiped out again with her hand. He dodged, but she let go of Az and swiped out at his exposed side. The Mortus screeched and fell to the ground, convulsing. The others paused to watch his death.

She met Godric's gaze across the room. His gray eyes were cold and...amused?

Dru gave the ring a final, desperate spin and grabbed Az again. *I just want to go somewhere safe. Like a Wayfarer's Hut. Preferably near stupid Set. And with our packs.*

They vanished.

CHAPTER 22

This time, Azrael didn't stumble.

But it was a close thing, thanks to the pack that had suddenly appeared at his feet. A very *familiar* pack.

Where the literal Hell are we now? The air held the tang of sulfur, so they were still in one of the three circles, but that didn't narrow things down. It was nighttime, but moonless. The area around them was bare of trees and shelter—just a few knee-high boulders decorating a gibber plain. A small timber cottage, complete with rock chimney, sat perched on the plain around a hundred yards away. It looked…quaint.

It probably turned into a giant chicken or something.

He brushed some of the dried blood from his wrists. "A bit of warning next time would be good."

Dru let go of his arm—immediately he missed her touch—and stepped back. She spotted a second backpack on the ground and prodded it thoughtfully with her toe.

"Really?" she said. "Did you want me to shout that we were about to teleport out of there? Give our enemies some warning?"

Her gray eyes spat fire—gone was the inky blackness—and her once-neat braid was mussed, strands of hair slipping free and caressing her cheekbones and plump lips. Her left cheek was smeared with a streak of blood, and her brows were drawn in a thunderous frown.

She was furious, all right, but she looked like a warrior princess of old; fierce, dangerous and powerful.

Blood rushed to his cock.

Not now.

Not ever, from the sounds of things. Who knew that she was toxic *there*? And she hadn't been lying about that, either. His lie-dar had detected no falsehood when she'd spoken.

That was probably why she didn't appreciate you coming onto her so hard at the ball. Had that only been a few days ago? It felt like months. And yeah. He shouldn't have done that. He'd clearly misread the signals, and he should apologize.

Later, though.

"Why are you staring at me like that?" she asked.

He wanted to adjust his straining erection, but that would draw her attention to his below-stairs discomfort. Who knew how she'd react in her current frame of mind? "No reason."

She put her hands on her hips. "We aren't going anywhere until you tell me what the Hell you were thinking about."

Well, all right… "You look pretty hot. That's all."

She snorted and turned away. "Like I'm buying that horseshit."

She dropped the subject. And then her jaw.

"What is it?" he asked.

"That is a *real* Wayfarer's Hut."

"A what-now?" The way she said it, it may as well have been all three pieces of Heaven's Heart, just sitting there waiting to be collected.

"A Wayfarer's Hut. They are meant to be a myth." She reached down, picked up her pack by its strap, then took a few tentative steps toward the timber structure.

"You sure it's what you think it is? What if it's a trap?"

She studied the area around the Hut. "Can't you feel it?"

"Feel what?"

"The peace here."

Peace? He hadn't felt peace since two of his comrades had been kidnapped and he'd been booted from Heaven. Then again, being a warrior in Heaven hadn't exactly been a settled existence anyway.

"You *don't* feel it?"

"I didn't say anything." Although, his lack of response had no doubt been answer enough.

"The air here, it's different." She inhaled deeply. "There's a sense of calmness that doesn't exist in any part of Hell I've ever visited. It's as though the aggression beneath the surface has been removed."

Truth.

All truth.

He stood, waiting to see if he could sense what she did, but all he got was the quiet. No animal sounds, no descending hordes, nothing. Just the scent of sulfur and the irritating buzz that Hell produced for someone like him.

Fallen, but not *truly* fallen.

"Maybe it's because I'm an angel," he said quietly.

Those clear gray eyes of hers stared straight through him, like they could see into his soul. "Possibly. Different rules for the 'good guys', I guess."

"So, what's the deal with a Wayfarer's Hut?" He grabbed his pack and slung it over his shoulder.

"They're safe places for travelers in Hell, to give them a night or two's rest before heading back into the fray. No violence can be dealt inside one; it's spelled to prevent it. And they only appear to those in need." She started toward the Hut.

Maybe it wasn't going to turn into something sinister and try to kill them, after all.

"Then how'd you find this one?"

"I asked the ring to transport us to my room in the guild, but it didn't work. So, then I asked for a Wayfarer's Hut, somewhere near Set."

Azrael's pulse accelerated at the former god's name. "Do you think we might be close to him?"

A shrug. "It's possible—the ring sent us to a Hut, after all."

"But not your room back at the guild." Which was interesting, and slightly worrying. Did the ring have a mind of its own?

He stared into the darkness that surrounded the plain, but aside from a sea of stars overhead nothing was visible.

The constellations are all wrong. Nothing like the Human Realm or Heaven's, at any rate. Funny how there hadn't been any in the sky outside the Mortus' den.

Dru waved a hand at the wooden dwelling. "Shall we go take a look?"

"Do you think anyone else might be there?"

"There's no glow in the windows."

That was true, and the air was free of wood smoke. But some demon species had excellent night vision, and others didn't feel the cold or need to cook, so something *could* be lurking in the shadows.

"Even if there is someone here," Dru said as she stepped onto the small porch, "they can't hurt us."

"I wouldn't be convinced of that." Sure, *she* believed in the anti-violence spells, but that didn't mean that they worked.

The handle turned easily in Dru's palm, and then they were inside. Azrael's acute vision pierced the gloom of the Hut easily—it was one large room with a hearth, couch, and table. There were some shelves up against the rear wall, but other than that the place was sparsely furnished. Two doors led off from the main area to his right.

He dropped his pack on the floor near the door. "Simplistic, but it has its own charm, I guess." As if in answer, a fire sprung to life in the hearth, a fierce glow emanating into the room. "Whoa."

Dru shot him an indecipherable look. "I'll check out one of the rooms, see if it's occupied. You do the same with the other door."

He gave her a mock salute, then silently crossed to the furthest door. *Is it a bathroom or bedroom?* Knocking would probably be best, either way. He didn't want to accidentally walk in on some demon having sex or jerking off. Both would be extremely awkward.

A gentle tap. No acknowledgement.

Opening the door, all his senses on alert, he almost sighed in disappointment to find a surprisingly well-appointed—and empty—bathroom. In fact, it made the rest of the Hut look dingy: marble tiles soared to the ceiling, there was a sunken bath with mosaic decorations, and a showerhead that looked designed for gods.

"This room is clear," he called out.

He jumped as Dru said, "Same."

She'd snuck up on him.

"Wow. This bathroom is top notch."

"What's the other room like?"

"A bedroom with a king-sized bed and enough pillows to sink a ship." It sounded as if the pillows were a personal affront.

"The side rooms are decadent, but the main room is utilitarian..." Azrael spun on his heel, back toward the hearth, and froze.

Gone was the simple furniture, and in its place was a luxury leather couch, a spotless wooden table, and candelabra for days.

"Uhh…"

Dru let out a low whistle. "The Hut seems to be responding to us."

Great. The whole place was starting to get an 'illicit lovers' feel to it. From the candlelight, to the rug on the floor in front of the fire, to the bottle of wine that had appeared on the table. With two glasses.

Just what his libido *didn't* need. A love nest. With the sexiest woman he'd ever seen.

The things he could do with her on that rug…

No. Nope. Nup.

Dru had toxic lady parts. And if that wasn't enough, she still hadn't kissed him, and she owed him one as part of their deal. Although, he didn't really want her to make out with him because she had to. He wanted—no *needed*—her to do it because *she* wanted to.

And that is not going to happen.

Ever.

And it shouldn't. An angel and a cambion getting it on? Even if he did manage to find all three pieces of Heaven's Heart, that act alone would probably bar him from Heaven.

Worth it.

Maybe. But not for his friends…

Although, would it really affect them?

Keep trying to talk yourself into it. Slight problem though: even if you do decide you want to, Dru might have a very different opinion.

Which was a shame.

A damn shame.

CHAPTER 23

The legends hadn't said Wayfarer's Huts were able to change themselves to suit their visitors. And what did it say about her and Az that the Hut had created a lavish environment ripe for new lovers?

Her gaze stroked from the crackling fire and the large rug sprawled before it, to the glowing candelabra and the frosty bottle of expensive-looking champagne. Even the dented sideboard had been replaced with an immaculate wall-unit that held a variety of gleaming crystal glasses and a platter of delicious-looking fruit.

"What now?" Az asked.

Dru ran a hand over her hair and grimaced at the crackle of dried blood and gods-knew what else. "I'm going to use the bathroom."

The fallen angel waggled his eyebrows. "Need help washing your back?"

"No."

"Pity."

He so wasn't what she'd assumed angels would be like. Maybe losing his wings had changed him. Shaking her head, she carried her pack into the bathroom and closed the door.

No lock.

This Hut had some serious issues. She stared at the gleaming white door, but nothing appeared. Apparently, it wasn't necessary.

Sighing, she dumped her pack on the tiled floor and began stripping off her blood-encrusted clothing. She left it lying where it fell and turned to the shower. Then looked over her shoulder at the bath.

That sunken tub looked pretty amazing.

But you haven't showered in a few days…

Right. She'd rinse off in the shower, and then soak in the bath. That sounded like a decent compromise.

Stepping under the spray, however, she changed her mind. It felt amazing—like rain poured down directly from the gods. The water was the perfect temperature and pressure, and it smelled amazing—like jasmine flowers, her favorite perfume.

She scrubbed until her skin was raw, then washed her hair with the soaps that had appeared in a little niche in the wall. Done, she stepped out to find the largest, fluffiest towel she'd ever seen sitting on the vanity.

She dried off quickly, before noticing that her discarded clothing had been placed in a folded pile.

And it was clean.

She almost groaned in appreciation. Instead, she settled for a "Thank you, Hut."

Man, she needed to get a self-cleaning laundry service back at the guild.

Once she was dressed, she braided her wet hair and emerged from the bathroom. Az was standing in the main room, the contents of his backpack scattered over a mahogany table. Even blood-soaked and weary, he still looked good enough to eat.

Enough of that.

He was a means to an end. They'd use each other to get to Set, then she'd steal the Orb and that would be that. It didn't count that she'd actually started to like him—a lot. He'd stuck around and helped her where he could, and he hadn't treated her as if she was breakable—like a lot of demon males tended to. She wasn't sure if they did it because she was female, cambion, or both. Even when they learned she was an assassin, they assumed she couldn't take care of herself. Never mind that she'd been brought up in an environment especially designed to make her a killer.

Apparently, being half-human made her 'delicate'.

She snorted.

Az's head jerked up at the sound. "All done?"

"Yep, and it was glorious."

A wicked gleam entered his eye. "I bet."

He'd never wrapped her in cotton wool, not once. Instead, he'd pushed and pushed at her, forcing her to keep up with him. Or forcing himself to keep up with her.

"You going to get clean?" she asked.

He began packing away his belongings. "Yeah."

"What were you doing?"

"Just double-checking supplies. Your relatives sorted through my stuff. I'm missing a couple of spell powders."

Damn. She hadn't thought to look.

He shoved the last item away and zipped the pack up. "Be back soon."

Then he was gone, the door shutting softly behind

him.

Moving to the table, Dru pulled out a chair and sank down into the seat. It had been a long two days. Tugging her cellphone out the pocket of her pack, she sighed. No reception. Not that she'd expected it, but Hell was sometimes surprising as to where and when you could communicate with others. She hadn't bothered bringing a spell to call home, since she'd thought she'd be in and out and done in a matter of hours.

I want to blame Trick for this, but I think the fault is entirely mine.

She didn't like admitting when she was wrong, but this whole thing was way over her head. Az. The Orb. Set.

And Peony.

She rubbed her temples.

Peony was looking after an angel. A real one, with wings, like Az had once had.

He probably knows the bastard.

Probably. But she wasn't going to give away the guild's secret, not when her sister was trapped there, vulnerable. And Az had friends. She remembered the dark-skinned woman from the party, and the two men dressed in expensive suits. If Az had been with them, then they were no doubt *all* fallen angels.

How did so many fall at once?

Something wasn't right about the situation. Angels getting kicked out of Heaven was a rare event—for so many at one time…

What had Az and his friends *done*?

The door to the bathroom opened and Az emerged. His ebony hair was wet and slicked back, and his black shirt clung to his muscular torso in a horrible way.

Horrible because it highlighted his pecs and six pack, and made her blood heat and her breasts tingle.

It's just fatigue.

Yeah, yeah.

And she was a human saint.

"Want some champagne?" she blurted.

He paused, then set his pack by the bedroom door. "Why not?"

Dru reached out and grabbed the condensation-beaded bottle, then read the gold label: *Moete*—was it a rip-off brand? Maybe it was the Hut's attempt to match human norms, except it couldn't get it quite right.

Peeling off the foil at the top, she unwound the cage, and popped the cork with little ceremony. No point in wasting the bubbly by having it foam everywhere.

Az placed two champagne flutes on the table, and then sat opposite her.

"Are you sure we're safe here?"

"Let's see." Dru set the bottle aside, walked over to him and punched him.

Or tried to.

Intense pain wracked her skull before her arm ever made contact. Clutching her head, she collapsed on her ass.

"Holy Hell!"

When she opened her eyes, Az was crouched next to her, concern writ across his face.

"You okay?"

"That *hurt*." Worse than any pain she'd ever experienced. Well, that she could remember experiencing recently, at any rate.

Gentle hands cupped her cheeks as Az tilted her face

up. "Are you sure you're okay?"

Dru inhaled deeply, and the pain receded a bit more. "I'll be fine." She held up a hand and Az took it, hauling her to her feet. Unbalanced, she bumped into his body. *Warm. Hard.* They were the first things she noticed as she plastered herself against his chest.

Damn, he felt good. And smelled amazing, too. Like sandalwood and spice.

"Whoa, that must have hit you harder than I thought." With both hands on her shoulders, he eased her away, his deep blue eyes concerned.

Great. Now he might think I'm breakable, too.

She really didn't like the idea of that.

"All good, just was a bit off balance." In more ways than one, although she wasn't going to admit that to him. Not when he'd gone and got all worried.

Breaking eye contact, she frowned. The Hut was wavering between the luxurious paradise and a worn and dirty hostel. Flashes of grimy tables and plates came and went, along with a series of bunks. The temperature had also gotten chilly, fast.

Oops.

"Sorry, Hut. I just wanted to check if the rumors were true."

The room froze for a second, a weird amalgamation of dirty table with champagne bottle, roaring fire with filthy floorboards, and half couch-half bunk, before it snapped back to the lovers' den it had been previously. The air warmed as well, but a little cold gust licked at the nape of her neck, which she took as a warning to behave.

"What was that about?" Az asked, his low voice melting through her.

"I think the Hut was offended I attacked you after it put so much effort into making us feel welcome."

"I see."

She slipped out from under his touch and grabbed the champagne bottle and a glass, before heading to the couch. She sank into its cushions; even though it had appeared as a warped version of itself moments earlier, it was ridiculously comfortable.

"I could get used to this," she said, and poured herself a glass of the Moete.

Az sat next to her, holding out his flute. She filled it to the brim. Placing the bottle on the floor, she wriggled deeper into the couch, tucking her legs up underneath her. She'd never been a big drinker, but after surviving the last few days, she figured she deserved to enjoy life for a few moments.

Guilt-free.

Yeah, she wasn't so sure about that. But she could at least relax in front of a fire, with a handsome guy sitting next to her, and the knowledge that anyone who arrived at the cabin wouldn't be able to hurt them.

She closed her eyes at the first sip of the champagne. It was sweet, with a hint of tartness, and the bubbles fizzed nicely on her tongue. This was better than the stuff they'd served at some of the fancy guild parties she'd been to.

She'd just taken another sip when Az asked, "So, how do you feel about being related to that Godric guy?"

Dru sprayed her mouthful in an arc, spluttering. "*What?*"

CHAPTER 24

The firelight from the hearth caressed the planes and angles of Dru's face. She was painfully beautiful. Harsh and regal, like the princess he'd thought her before.

And now he knew how deadly she was.

It only made her more appealing, really.

Even if she had just spat out a mouthful of champagne across the room.

"*What*?"

"You're related to that Godric guy." Azrael had thought about it while he was in the shower. No other Mortus demon had gray eyes—not that he'd seen all of them—but Godric had been awfully interested in Dru's parentage. And there *had* been a similarity to their features, and the king's.

She wiped her mouth with the back of her hand. "That's a Hell of an assumption."

He outlined his theory, then took a long draw of his bubbly drink. Human alcohol was still a bit of a mystery to him. Yael had taken a keen interest in the stuff, but Azrael had spent most of his time undercover on missions, and he had wanted to keep his wits about him. Not that he was sure he could get drunk, anyway.

She frowned at the fire, thinking. "I guess it's possible. I don't know who my father was. He must have been mated to my mother, or he got her pregnant using a turkey baster or something, because she'd be dead otherwise. Humans can't survive a Mortus' touch."

There were a few interesting points there, but—"Turkey baster?"

She gave him a sideways glance. "You know, artificial insemination."

"No." Humans had babies like angels did—the old-fashioned way. At least, that's what he'd always assumed. However, he'd been warrior class his entire adult life. Maybe humans did stuff differently now.

They certainly did things the old-fashioned way with me.

When he'd first fallen, he'd managed to fuck his way through his share of women. None of them had wanted to get pregnant, though, and insisted on a condom. He hadn't bothered telling them that, as an angel, it was highly unlikely he'd father any offspring. He'd worn the hat, and the sex had still been good, especially for someone who'd been denied it their entire life.

He'd lived for the cause, after all.

"Uh, some humans artificially fertilize themselves, or get embryos implanted into their womb."

Science, the bane of the archangels' existence.

"Interesting." He couldn't help but admire the humans' ingenuity.

They sat in silence for a few moments, while the logs popped and crackled in the hearth. But no matter how long the fire burned, the wood never seemed to need topping up. He could get used to living in a place like this, even if it was sort of sentient.

"So, why'd you fall?" Dru's voice rang loudly in the room.

His whole body locked tight, and he had to will himself to relax. *It's only normal she'd want to know.* After all, she was a cambion who lived in a guild. She'd never have had much reason to come into contact with an angel before. And she'd have no idea how invasive her question was.

He took a sip, to delay a little, but found himself replying soon after. "I didn't fall. I was kicked out of Heaven."

Both her eyebrows rose. "Kicked *out*?"

"Yeah."

"Why?"

"It's complicated." He ran a hand over his half-dry hair.

She gave him a wry smile. "We have time."

Yeah, but I don't want to talk about it.

Except maybe he should. It wasn't like he had anyone to discuss this with. Yael, Seraphina and Raze didn't like the topic being brought up, not unless it related to finding Zadkiel and Dina. And it wasn't like he had any friends he could share it with, either. No one he'd known in Heaven had bothered to contact him, and he doubted they ever would. A normal angel wouldn't want to be tarnished by familiarity with one such as him.

"I was in an elite squadron called the Darts. We were tasked with guarding Heaven's Heart, one of our most treasured artifacts."

She narrowed her eyes, but didn't say anything, just

waved a hand in the air for him to continue.

"Six months ago, Heaven was raided while two of my team were on watch. The Heart was stolen, and my comrades abducted."

"And they kicked *you* out for it?"

Ouch. Dru really knew how to cut. Even though the verbal slice wasn't meant for him, it still hurt. They'd been used as scapegoats, and he'd understood that, even as Uriel had sliced off his wings.

"The break-in was considered to be a security failing on our part."

She rolled her eyes. "So, the rest of Heaven's army wasn't responsible? How'd they break in? Who was it?"

"I don't know. Demons, we think."

"What happened to your wings?"

"The archangels cut them off." He didn't know what they'd done with them after. Maybe hung them up for all to see, as a lesson on what failure would cost.

She winced, her fingers tightening on the stem of the flute. "Did it hurt?"

He looked down at his legs. "Worse than anything I could imagine. Although, your toxin was almost as bad."

She bit her lip at that. "I'd say I was sorry, but I'm not. You deserved it."

Yeah, he probably had at the time.

It was helping, telling her this; like lancing a boil. The rage and despair oozed from a wound he hadn't known he had, or cared to examine too closely, at any rate.

"I hope that archangel's wings rot off."

Azrael choked on his drink. Once he could breathe again, he shook his head. "You shouldn't say that!"

"We're in Hell. They cut off your wings and used you

as an excuse. Unless…you didn't let those demons into Heaven, did you?" Her gray eyes went wide.

"*No.*"

She settled back into the sofa. "I didn't think so."

"Sad that I have a demon on my side, when no other unfallen angel is."

"What's wrong with having a demon agree with you? We may not be the 'good guys', but we're honest when we screw someone over. Sounds like your archangel buddies couldn't give a fuck what happens to you."

He winced. "They're archangels. They know stuff I am not privy to."

At least, that's what he'd always been told. And he'd believed it, drunk that Kool-Aid down *and* asked for seconds.

She poured herself another glass. "Did they at least give you a way to earn your wings back?"

"Yes. Find Heaven's Heart and return it to them."

"Well, that shouldn't be too hard."

He sighed. "Except there's apparently three pieces, and Heaven only held *one*. They want all three of them."

She lowered the bottle to the ground, slowly. "You mean they want you to find two extra pieces that no other angel has been able to locate in centuries?"

"Yes."

"Sounds like a fool's bargain." A dark shadow flickered across her face.

"That's because it is."

"Then why agree to it?"

"Who said I agreed?"

She arched an eyebrow. "You're saying you didn't?"

"No, we did." Because they'd felt they could win at

the time. In pain and in shock, they probably would have agreed to anything. Not that they'd had any real choice in the matter, though.

"You and those other three."

So, she'd seen them at the party.

He nodded.

"Why are you doing assassination work, then?"

"It pays the bills."

"I feel like there's a missing 'and' at the end of that sentence."

"And it helps me track down leads. We're trying to find our two missing comrades and the Heart at the same time. It's why I took the job for Set. We want Odin's Orb."

She was silent for a long moment. "Odin's Orb?"

"Yeah. I don't know much about it, other than the rest of the crew want it." He shrugged.

"And do you know where your buddies got taken?"

He shook his head, gut burning at the thought. "No clue. But we will find them, and destroy whoever took them."

Something danced across her features, but it was gone in a heartbeat. "If I wasn't enslaved, I'd help you."

"Wait, you're *still* enslaved?" He bit the side of his cheek.

"Yeah, I told you, I was sold into blood-slavery."

"But you said you had a 'boss'…"

"Euphemism."

Anger built up inside his chest, his heart pounding in his ears. How could he have failed to put two and two together? That Dru was *still* a slave—it was wrong. That *anyone* could be sold into slavery was wrong, but that this strong woman hadn't managed to free herself yet…

"Can you get your freedom?"

"Once I've worked off my debt. This mission, if I succeed, should go a long way toward that."

They were silent for a while.

It felt good, to have shared their stories, but something about it didn't feel quite right…He grabbed the bottle of Moete from the floor and read the back label.

Full-bodied and rich with flavor, this bottle has a distinctive sweetness, echoed by citrussy overtones. Notes of nutmeg are also apparent in the rich overlay of sensation. 20 per cent alcohol. May contain truth serum.

He began laughing.

"What?"

Dru snatched the bottle from him and cursed when she reached to the end of the description. "That sneaky Hut." But her expression was almost admiring, as she glanced around the room.

It made him want to kiss her.

Rather desperately.

"So," he blurted. "What about our deal?"

CHAPTER 25

"Deal?" Dru echoed.

Azrael had leaned closer while she'd re-read the bottle's label, the scent of sandalwood making her mouth water. She drew in a deep breath, savoring the taste of it on her tongue. *Even better than the champagne.*

His voice cut through her thoughts. "You know, where you owe me a kiss."

A bucket of cold water couldn't have woken her up more quickly. "Oh. *That.*"

He drew back as if she'd stung him.

How could she have forgotten about that stupid bargain? She'd just assumed she'd weasel her way out of it, somehow. But it had been a bargain with an angel. Those things were binding.

"So, you want me to kiss you because of our deal?" She hadn't meant to sound so uncertain.

"No, I want you to kiss me because you want to. But we do have that deal." He almost sounded…bashful.

Well, didn't that just mess things up. It meant that if she kissed him because it was her choice, then she hadn't fulfilled the terms of their deal. But if she kissed him because of their bargain, it would imply she didn't want him…

And Hell help her, she *wanted* him.

She didn't want to want him, but she did. And the way her life had been going the last few days, this might be her only chance to actually *have* him. Before he went back to his friends, before she stole Odin's Orb right out from under him and he never forgave her…

You are such a jerk.

Yes, she was. Because she needed that Orb to appease Trick, and she had to earn both hers and Peony's freedom before her sister was drawn too deeply into the underbelly of their world. Az wouldn't understand, not when his wings were on the line, but she had to watch out for herself and her sister. No one else was going to. And it wasn't like Trick was going to *help* her earn her debt off.

Technically, she didn't *owe* Az anything.

Finders keepers.

Yeah, that wasn't minimizing the guilt that was threatening to choke her.

But a deal was a deal, even a stupid one, and she was feeling a little reckless. Maybe the champagne label should have read 'dangerous to drinkers' rather than all that gumph about flavors and spells.

She set the glass on the floor, then reached over and grabbed his hand. He let her take it, the tightening around his mouth the only indication he was wary of her intentions.

"I won't claw you," she said, running a finger over his inner wrist. His skin felt soft, and she marveled at the sensation—at the trust he showed by not pulling free from her grip.

His blue eyes darkened. "It's not like you haven't done that before."

"Plan on taking what isn't being given freely?" She met his gaze.

"No." His voice was rough as he stared at her meandering finger.

"Then you have nothing to worry about." Pulling his hand toward her, she raised it to her mouth, so that her breath fanned across his skin. She licked her lower lip, imagining pressing her mouth just *there*. He inhaled sharply.

"*This* is for the deal." She placed a hot, wet kiss on the back of his hand.

Az froze, barely breathing, watching her with smokey blue eyes as she flicked her tongue out, tasting him, before lifting her head. *Delicious.*

He grunted, although he didn't pull his hand away. "You cheated."

"You never said where." She gave him a wicked smile.

"No, I guess I didn't."

They sat there like that for a moment, holding hands. Then he tugged, drawing her slowly toward him. She went, her heartbeat speeding up.

His voice was low. "Can I ask you a favor?"

They were close now, barely inches apart. The heat emanating from his rock-hard body, and the sandalwood scent of him were mesmerizing. She stared at his mouth, wondering if it would feel as soft as it looked...

"What would that be?" she asked, so close that when she spoke, their lips almost brushed in a pseudo-kiss.

Like the first time they met, but this was so much hotter. Sexier. Warmth pooled between her thighs at the thought of kissing him properly. Freely.

A wicked gleam danced in his azure eyes. "Could we make out for a little bit?"

Surprise had her grip on his hand tightening, then she chuckled, the breathy sound strange to her ears. "For a little bit."

She had other plans, but she didn't get a chance to voice them. His mouth slammed down on hers, hot and firm, tongue mischievously grazing the seam of her lips. Aside from their mouths and hands, which were still clasped, they didn't touch.

It didn't matter.

Fuck.

He tasted like the champagne, but headier, more delicious. She moaned, opening her mouth, greedily seeking with her own tongue, enjoying the silken slide as it clashed with his. Hungry for more, she raised her free hand, clenching it on his shoulder. He looped an arm around her waist, lifting her like she weighed nothing, and deposited her on his lap. She straddled his thighs, the position pressing her core against his erection, which hit her in just the right spot.

She groaned.

She'd never felt anything so good before. Ever.

In response, he grabbed her braid in one hand, tilting her head to the side, his tongue mimicking sex in an erotic hint at her future.

She pulled away, panting, and ground herself against his straining cock. Her body ached for him. "Can we do more than make out?" she asked, breathless.

"I think we already are," he said, lips wet and eyes a little crazed.

It was the sexiest thing she'd ever seen.

"Mmmm." She lowered her mouth to his neck, sucking hard against his pounding pulse.

"Fuck." His head fell back against the sofa's cushion, and his hips thrust upward, pressing against her with every undulating sweep.

So good.

She couldn't remember the last time she'd wanted anyone the way she did this fallen angel. And the *feel* of him against her. She shut her eyes and bit down gently on his neck. His responding moan was low, agonized.

This is amazing, and we haven't even hit second base.

Like he could read her thoughts, he freed his hands, skimming one of them over her ribs, the other pulling out the tie to her braid. Her heart pounded in anticipation as her hair fell loose around her. One of his thumbs met the underside of a breast and he gave a single, gentle stroke, before his mouth met hers again; hungry, wet, demanding. Desire shot through her at the fleeting touch, and she kissed him back, needing him, needing *more*.

She pushed her chest toward his body, arching into his hand as he finally cupped her breast, his fingers sliding over an aching nipple. He withdrew from the kiss. "I want to suck these." He stroked her again, the pleasure intense.

Pulling away slightly, she jerked her shirt off, then her bra, before leaning in to swirl her tongue over his earlobe as she ground herself against his length, the friction making her core throb, empty. Her breasts pressed against his chest, the added contact making her gasp.

He moaned, stroking her again. "You're freaking perfect."

"You're wearing clothes. Why are you wearing clothes?"

He gave her a rusty chuckle, then his shirt joined hers on the floor, and he began lazily kissing his way down her neck.

The slight licks and suction were electrifying. She slid her hands over his chest, greedy for the feel of him. The caramel expanse of his skin was so smooth and sexy, his six-pack defined even though they were half sprawled on the sofa.

Then his mouth was on her breast.

"Ohhhh."

She hadn't ever experienced foreplay like this before—heady, sweet, and intense all at the same time. Dru wanted to feel all of him, lick every inch of his perfect body. But she doubted she'd have the patience. She wanted him inside her, to know what it was like to have him brand her with his passion, and him with hers.

He pulled away slightly, then nipped the side of her breast, the tiny bite of pain delicious. "I don't think we should keep this up."

"Oh? You don't feel like you're having any problems." She slid a hand down his abdomen, then lower, to cup his erection. His cock was hot and hard in her palm, and her fingers struggled to close.

She needed to taste him, to *feel* him.

He arched into her palm as she slowly stroked her hand up, then down. His voice was strained. "You said make out. Not fuck. Also, you're uh, lady parts, are, uh, deadly."

She squeezed his cock lightly, delighting in the sound of his breath hitching. "But you survived my toxin already."

"True."

"So, you *should* be immune." She wasn't sure who she needed to convince more—him or herself.

"What if I'm not?"

"I think you are." Well, she sure as Hell hoped he was.

She wasn't ready for this to end. She needed to experience *more*. With him.

Only him.

He gave her a smile then, heart-wrenching in its sweetness. "It'd be a good way to die."

Her hand stopped its movement. Dru forced the words out, "We don't have to have sex."

His hand stroked her jawline, while the other slid down to cup between her legs, the contact searing in its intensity. "Yeah, I think we do. I might go insane if we don't."

His words didn't register at first, her body focused on the pleasure of his touch. How her body *ached* in response. Then she realized what he'd said.

Thank the gods.

She climbed off his lap and reached out to the waistband of his pants. Kneeling in front of him—feeling vulnerable but also powerful—she undid the zipper, slowly. So slowly. He lifted his hips, helping her slide off his cargos.

Good gods. He was commando.

His cock sprang up, freed from its confines. She eyed the hard length of him, panties growing damper. "I guess they build angels well up there. Who knew?"

"My eyes are up here." Az ran a hand over his mouth then took his cock in his hand and began stroking, teasing her.

Her eyes locked on his movements, her fingers itching to replace his. But the view so was erotic, that she couldn't move, could barely breathe.

His eyes were heavy-lidded. "Are you just going to watch?"

Without thinking, she slid her hands up the inside of his thighs, and then grasped his cock. She needed to taste him, feel him in her mouth. Greedy, she licked over the slick crown, before drawing it deep into her mouth, moaning around his shaft. She couldn't take it all the way in, so she used her hand to stroke at the base, while another cupped his balls. She sucked at his cock like she was starving, the flavor of him like hot spices.

"Mmm." Placing a gentle hand on the back of her head, he thrust into her mouth. It was hot. So fucking hot. Then he eased her away from his cock, and she reluctantly released it. The length glistened in the firelight, and she licked her lips, wanting more. "I thought the goal was for us to have sex, not you blow me."

"Can't we do both?"

His voice was rough. "Not right now."

Suddenly she was airborne, lifted and deposited onto her back on the plush rug by the fire. Her pants were gone, and she was bare except for her underwear. He leaned over her, running a finger over her mound. "You're so wet already. I bet you taste delicious."

She arched into his touch, wanting more of it, of *him*. "You're a good kisser."

He slid up the length of his body, fusing his mouth to hers as his fingers worked their way under her panties. The feel of him there, the smooth glide of his fingers over her pussy, it had her burning on the inside. She'd never felt this *connection* before, so intense she was sure she'd come from his hands alone.

"I'm still alive." Then her panties were gone, and his fingers were thrusting deep, just where she needed it. Needed *him*. "Come for me."

She panted, her head pressed back against the rug. His thumb found her clit and her whole body exploded in ecstasy, her orgasm catching her by surprise. Her body milked his fingers with strong contractions, and she could hear him curse next to her ear as bliss threatened to overwhelm her.

Before she'd calmed, he withdrew his hand and moved, coming to kneel between her legs. His cock pressed against her in an intimate caress, and she watched as he licked her wetness from his fingers, closing his eyes as he sucked on them. "Fuck."

She thrust her hips, wanting him inside her *now*, but he pulled back slightly. Did she taste as good to him as he did to her? He withdrew his fingers, then lowered his hands to either side of her head. "Dru, are you sure?"

She met his blue gaze, saw the desire there, and the need. But he waited. For *her*.

"Yes."

He thrust forward, sliding his entire length into her in one hot, glorious movement.

Her mind went completely blank. She didn't think she'd ever experienced anything so delicious. She *knew* she hadn't. Because even though she wasn't a virgin, her partners had all died quickly after entering her. Whereas Az…

He'd frozen above her.

Her eyes opened and she stared at him, panic clawing at her, drowning out the heady passion. "Are you okay?"

His black hair hung down, framing his jaw, which was clenched tight. He then dropped a kiss to her forehead. "Yes, are you?"

She grinned. "You didn't die."

"Not yet."

"If you were going to, you would have already."

"I don't know," he said, withdrawing slightly, before sliding forward sharply. Her whole body sang in response. "This just might kill me anyway."

His body within hers, it felt…*right.* She held her breath at each glide of his length, her body coiling tighter and tighter with building pleasure. She rolled her hips, grinding upwards to catch her clit against the base of his cock with each thrust.

Az's face became pinched, his movements jerky. "I need to come."

"Do it." She was panting, her heart thundering in time with his.

"But—"

"Do it!" She bit down on his shoulder.

He went wild, thrusting against her so that she slid across the floor, his hands holding her hips tightly, pinning her for his onslaught as he sought their pleasure. His loss of control…The intensity made her shatter, fragmenting into a million pieces. The orgasm went on and on as he exploded deep within her, and she came again as she felt the hot rush of his orgasm. She clung to him, barely able to breathe through the ecstasy.

The heavy weight of him pressed against her, their heartbeats pounding against one another as she trembled in lingering pleasure. Az lifted himself away, but left his hips firmly pressed against hers. Bewilderment suffused his face, and she reached up a hand to stroke his jaw. Even then, he was so handsome it made her heart hurt. "That was amazing."

She bit down on her lip. "I know."

And it probably wasn't ever going to happen again.

Strangely, for the first time in decades, she felt the urge to cry. But she wasn't going to ruin this moment, not with a stupid burst of emotion. It didn't matter that this was the closest she'd ever been to another living being, that she'd had the best sexual experience of her life.

Or that he was immune to her.

Once they'd done the job with Set, this would all be over. She'd have to go back to her life, and forget that this fallen angel had rocked her world, reset it. That she actually liked him—*way too much*—and could see that. what they had was special.

Rare.

He bumped her nose with his. "Do you think we should try it again? To see if it was a fluke?"

His cock was still hard.

Shoving aside the unwanted gloom, she lifted her hips, hissing at the feel of him sliding within her, desire thrumming through her. "Why not?"

After all, what was the worst thing that could happen?

CHAPTER 26

They were soaking in the enormous tub, the scent of jasmine wreathing the air.

He'd never felt so relaxed in his life. His arms were like wet noodles, and his bones weak, like he'd been drained dry. But it was fantastic.

Dru's wet hair was plastered to the sides of her face, her golden skin illuminated by the candelabra that had appeared in the bathroom when they'd decided it was time to clean up. She, too, looked exhausted but content.

Azrael wondered how he was going to manage keeping her a secret from the others. Not that he was ashamed of her; skies, she was more likely to be ashamed of him, a fallen angel with no wings who'd been booted out of Heaven to preserve its reputation. No, he wanted to keep her a secret because he was sure the others wouldn't understand.

Demons were the enemy, after all.

"I could stay in this tub forever," Dru said into the drowsy silence.

He floated over to her, wrapping an arm around her

shoulders. She tensed for a moment, then relaxed into his embrace. "Same."

She drew a circle on his forearm with her finger. "I have to complete my mission."

He resisted the urge to move away from her. Her mission was to kill Set; his was to kill Set and take the Orb. He was happy to let her have half of it. "Same."

"I'm sorry for what happened to you and your friends." Her voice was soft.

"It's not your fault."

She'd spoken nothing but truth to him this evening, and he was grateful for it. Her honesty was refreshing. Even the other Darts had lied to him from time to time, which was strange, because they'd known he could sense it.

Then again, everyone was entitled to their privacy.

A loud crash jerked them to alertness.

Dru shoved her damp hair back from her face. "What was that?"

It sounded again, like a fist on wood. He frowned. "I think it might be the front door."

"Someone's here?" Her expression turned grim.

"We know the peace spell works. You finish washing up and I'll see who's there."

And draw them away from the Hut and kill them, if need be.

From the look on her face, she guessed at the direction of his thoughts. "I can do it."

"I know."

That seemed to mollify her, and she sank back into the water until it lapped at her chin.

He climbed out the tub and threw on some clothes,

then shut the bathroom door behind him with a click. He tucked his shirt into his pants as he walked across the main room to the door, where the banging was increasing in tempo and frequency.

He wasn't really interested in talking to the building, but he'd heard Dru do it, and it had appeared to respond. "Hut: if they're bad, zap them."

The air seemed to charge a little in response.

Azrael unlocked the door and let it swing inward. His jaw dropped in surprise.

"*Yael*?"

His comrade from the Darts stood on the threshold, wearing a pair of faded blue jeans, a black turtleneck, and a pissed off expression. "Finally. What took you so long to answer the door?"

Yael pushed past him into the Hut, and the air sparked in warning.

Azrael looked around, not sure where to direct his words. He settled on the hearth. "He's a friend."

The atmosphere calmed.

"Who are you talking to?" Yael asked. He was kitted out with a military grade backpack and was covered in weapons. He'd have many more that weren't visible too, but Azrael knew they'd be there. Yael never went anywhere without at least three daggers, a gun, and a garrote.

"The Hut."

Yael dropped his pack to the floor. "I always knew you were a few screws loose."

Love you too, buddy.

"This is a Wayfarer's Hut. It's kind of sentient."

"Huh."

"You don't believe me."

"No, not really."

"Well, you should." Dru's voice speared through the room. Yael slowly pivoted to face her, his expression blank as he took in the white hair, golden skin and black clothes.

"Isn't this the woman who sliced you up and left you for dead?"

Azrael rocked back on his heels, shoving his hands in his pockets. "Yep."

"Then why is she here now?"

Her gray eyes resembled crystals of frost. "Because we teamed up."

"Why?" Distrust narrowed Yael's eyes.

"Because we got into a spot of bother on the mission," Azrael said. "And two of us were better than one."

"I figured you'd had some problem with Set," Yael said, his gaze locked on Dru. "But it doesn't excuse this." He waved a hand, indicating the two of them together.

Probably a good thing he didn't—and wouldn't—know that they'd just had the most amazing sex ever.

"Yeah? I didn't think I needed your permission about how I did my jobs, so long as they got done."

"We got worried. You didn't check in."

"I didn't know I had to. And I couldn't." Azrael tapped the side of his head. He wasn't sure why, but when he tried reaching his mind out again he still couldn't find Seraphina or Raze.

Yael?

Yeah?

Can you reach the others?

A pause.

No.

Yael continued speaking, like their mental chitchat hadn't happened. "Well, when we heard nothing from you for days, I tried tracing you with the spell I snuck into your pack. but you kept bouncing all over the place, even went off the grid a couple of times. This was the first time we actually got a lock on you."

They had *tracked* him? Azrael told himself not be insulted, but for fuck's sake. They hadn't thought he was up to the task?

Yeah, he *was* insulted.

"Why did you put a tracer on me?"

"You weren't one hundred per cent when you left. Because of *her*." Yael nodded at Dru, who gave him the finger.

"Considering he's over it, you should try and build a bridge," she said.

"Why would I build a bridge? What has human infrastructure got to do with this?"

She looked at Yael like he was an idiot or from a totally different planet. "Uh, so you could get over it?"

Azrael could tell their little debate was about to devolve, so he cut in. "I took the mission. I was fine."

"Clearly not, if a bloody demon gave you some trouble. Two demons now." Yael gestured at Dru.

"Set is a former *god*, he's not a regular demon," Azrael said. He'd learned that the hard way. His pride and the sense of superiority he'd been taught in Heaven had been his undoing there. He'd seriously underestimated his foe.

"Deposed god."

"Still a god," Dru snapped.

"So how did you get here?" Azrael asked, redirecting

the conversation. Dru looked like she'd happily slice-and-dice Yael if given half the chance.

The guy *was* a smartass.

"Teleported."

"How?"

"By spending a lot of money."

Azrael assumed he should feel guilty about that, but considering how much cash he'd brought in since becoming an assassin, well, he figured he'd probably paid the bill already, and then some.

"You can just go home now and let me finish this," he said.

"That would be a no. Unless you've killed Set and we can leave already."

"He's still alive." As far as Azrael knew, anyway. With the contract that Hades had out on him, the sorcerer could very well be a corpse by now. And the Orb might be gone.

He wasn't going to mention that to Yael. The others already doubted his abilities.

"Then we should go."

Dru shook her head. "That was the problem last time. We rushed in with no plan. This time has to be different."

Yael took a looming step toward her. "There is no more 'we', not now that I'm here."

She smiled, a cold expression that promised pain, but her eyes didn't turn black. Not yet, anyway. "Az and I have a deal. You weren't part of it."

Yael looked over his shoulder and mouthed, "Az?"

He didn't rise to the bait. "She's right. Set is powerful, and his stronghold is warded to the hilt. He also happens to have a dragon guarding his treasure room. We work as a team. All *three* of us."

"A *dragon*?"

"Yes. They love a good hoard," Dru said. She gave Azrael a look that said, 'How do you put up with this guy?'

"Fine. She can come with us. But if she gets in the way, I'm not going to hold back."

Azrael stepped up to Yael, forcing his friend to face him. "You won't hurt her."

"If she interferes in our mission—"

"Aww, it's nice to be fought over and all, but here's a bit of news." Dru sidled up to Yael and rested her claws against his cheek. "Az is immune to my toxin, but I don't know if you are." Azrael looked down: as well as unsheathing her claws, she now had a knife pressed to Yael's chest. "Either way, the only reason you aren't dead right now is because this Hut is spelled to prevent violence."

Yael's jaw clenched hard, and a tick started at his left eye as the reality of his situation sank in. He was *furious.*

"Dru is an assassin," Azrael said. "She is a benefit to our team, not a hindrance."

"She works for a rival guild. She'll screw us over."

"Fine. Whoever gets to Set first, kills him. That clear enough?" he asked.

"Fine," Yael said, his anger shrinking as realized the implications of the deal. Dru could have Set; they were after the Orb. "First in, first served. Now, how do we kill this motherfucker?"

CHAPTER 27

They were back inside Set's castle.

The perimeter wall had been decorated with several bodies since their escape. Dru figured they were all the assassins who'd been sent after the god. She hadn't wanted to look at the remains too closely, but it seemed a number of them had been chewed on. *Probably the dragon.*

At least, she hoped it had been the dragon, otherwise it meant that something else within the castle liked the taste of flesh.

The wards had been super-charged, too, so their entrance had needed a little creative thinking. In the end, it had been Hermes' ring that had solved that problem. The emerald had flared to life not long after they'd entered Set's lands, and a single thought later, they were in.

Yael had tried to get her to take the ring off, so he could 'inspect' it, but it wouldn't budge. It was like it had been glued to her finger with magic.

I'll probably have to die to get rid of it.

But that wasn't a bad thing. Teleportation was handy,

even if it was a little unpredictable at times.

"Where are we?" Az asked.

"Back where I first came in," Dru said. She'd figured it was probably the safest place, since the treasure room had its own dragon.

"That doesn't tell us anything," Yael hissed.

Man, she really didn't like Az's buddy. Sure, he was a fallen angel, and had had his wings robbed, if the story Az had told her was true. But the guy was an arrogant prick, and she'd had to deal with her unfair share of those over the years.

Sure, she might be a demon, but that didn't make her scum.

According to Yael's judgmental stare, it did.

It's a good thing I'll never see Az again. His friends clearly wouldn't approve of me.

Her chest ached at the thought of the angel walking out of her life.

Deciding her silence had irritated Yael enough, she nodded her head toward a passage. "This way."

Together, the trio shadowed through the castle, careful to avoid any traps. Yael had arrived with a handy ointment that let them see magic, and the two angels had turned both themselves and her invisible to the outside world—although they could still see each other.

Having Az's and Yael's blood smeared on her chest was an experience she would prefer never to repeat, however. Yael had touched her that little bit too long, so as to make the whole thing uncomfortable and her claws itchy. But she hadn't cut him up, and they were all working together, at least for now.

The doors to the treasure room stood open as they

approached.

"Should we go this way again?" Dru asked.

Az frowned at the entrance. "It's in the middle of the castle. There's no other way but to go through."

"Surely there's a servants' hallway or something."

"Not on any map I've seen. And we don't have a lot of time to spend looking for it."

She nodded in agreement. The invisibility spell had a short life expectancy.

"Through the treasure chamber it is."

They separated slightly, each one creeping through the maze of cabinets. She spotted Yael standing frozen before a glass case filled with large white feathers.

"Don't touch anything," she warned.

He flashed an irritated look, but kept walking, tension riding in his shoulders. The feathers had really seemed to bother him.

Not my problem.

They were halfway through the labyrinth—Dru gave the swirling glow of lights from her first visit a wide berth—before she caught the sound of scales slithering on stone. She froze, holding up her arm with a closed fist, so that Az and his buddy could see. Everyone stopped.

A long, serpentine tail flickered in her peripheral vision. Gold and green glinted in the dim light cast by the display cabinets, and a low hiss reverberated through the chamber.

There weren't a lot of things that fazed her, but a goddamn dragon was one. Highly intelligent, viciously protective, and with a mouth that could swallow her whole—yeah, she was right to be wary, even if she was invisible.

The tail slithered out of sight.

She lowered her arm.

They moved on.

Dried blood was on the stone floor further ahead, within the markings of another Devilsnare, and she saw smears of ash and grease in the shape of a body in its center. Another dead assassin.

Or just someone who had annoyed Set.

Another minute, and they were through the treasure room, and into another hallway. This one had walls lined with glittering gold panels, heavily engraved with hieroglyphs. She had no idea what the symbols meant, but recognized Set's cartouche, complete with the Set animal and a dude with a beard. According to her initial research—okay, a quick check of Wikipedia—the Set animal was a mythical creature, but she'd seen those critters before in Hell. They were like the Reynard's Imps; vicious hunters, despite their furry and weirdly cute appearance.

Az took the lead, and they followed him down the hallway. No doors were apparent— although the decorated panels might hide hidden entrances—until they reached a large gold doorway at the end of the corridor. It was open.

Yael moved past Az, staring through the narrow opening into the space beyond. He was silent for a moment before nodding, then disappearing inside.

Dru moved up next to Az. He leaned down, so that his mouth brushed against the shell of her ear. "Remember: whoever gets there first."

She nodded. Too bad he didn't realize that applied to the Orb as well.

Then Az was through the door.

She bit the inside of her cheek, then took a deep breath. "First there," she muttered to herself and stepped across the threshold.

The room stretched for three hundred yards, ending in a large golden throne. More display cabinets were visible either side of the elaborate seat. Pillars of sandstone soared upward, giving the space a desert vibe.

It looks like a temple from Egypt.

Set had really taken his role of god seriously.

Slipping through the room silently, she spotted Yael and Az near the throne. Light, blinding in its intensity, seared her eyes as she reached them, pain shooting through her. She was desperate to rub her eyes to ease the burn, get her vision back; instead she held up her hands, claws out.

If they were going to be attacked, now would be the time.

Dru spun toward a low growl to her left, but a sledgehammer hit her in the gut, sending her flying. She slammed to a stop against one of the pillars, sliding down its length to the cold stone floor. Something in her spine protested, but she didn't stay down for long.

Being a cambion had some benefits.

She blinked rapidly, relief pouring through her as cloudy shapes began to form in her vision. Her eyesight was returning.

"Didn't you learn the last time?" Set's voice slithered through the room. Clearly, they were no longer invisible.

Damn it. Their advantage was gone.

Back on her feet, she hurried to Az and Yael, who were now engaged in hand-to-hand against two large demons.

Envoi demons—nasty bastards with poisonous horns. Set stood on his own next to his throne, the light catching on his dark brown skin, golden silk clothes and dazzling ruby eyes.

She turned toward the former god. "We got away last time," she said.

His mouth flattened into a thin line, the bones of his face sharpening, growing more predatory. "Because you stole something from me."

"Stole, borrowed…semantics."

Az grunted and slid a dagger through the stomach of his Envoi, but that didn't slow it down too much. Yael just looked intense and…happy.

I really don't like that guy.

Sure, she was an assassin, but it's not like she enjoyed the killing. Most of the time.

"Does the ring come off?" Set asked, watching her with a reptilian expression as she approached.

"No. Want to try?" She sprinted forward; he swept a sword at her and she ducked low.

Where the Hell had he hidden that?

She swiped her claws at his legs, scoring through the silk and slicing flesh, then rolled out of range. She paused, waiting for the god to collapse. *I'll cut his head off then.*

Something slammed into her from behind, and she hit the ground hard. Her breath was knocked out of her lungs with a whoosh, and she struggled for air, to relax, to just *breathe.*

Above her, Az arched in pain, a grunt escaping his clenched jaw.

Set stood behind him, sword spearing him through the

back.

No.

"Az!"

He was an angel, he could survive this.

He had to.

The smell of burning metal rose in the air, the scent disturbing and frightening. What was happening?

Then Set's glittering gaze met hers. "You think your little toxin would work on me? I am a *god!*"

CHAPTER 28

"A dead god."

A shadow loomed behind the deity, and the light caught on a slashing blade, then Azrael saw Yael watching dispassionately as Set's head fell to the stone floor below with a wet thump.

Black blood spurted in an arc, raining down on Az and Dru, splattering Yael in the face.

The sword jerked in Az's back and he twisted to pull himself from the blade.

It emerged, the end half-dissolved.

Az breathed through the pain. He'd recover from the wound, provided the blade hadn't been coated in toxin. He was furious he'd let his guard slip enough to get stabbed, but he hadn't been willing to watch the god kill Dru. She'd had the deity at her mercy, but paused for some reason, as if waiting for something to happen, and Set had been closer to her than she'd realized—there'd been two of him, one an illusion. The god had been readying for the killing blow.

"Are you okay?" Dru was beside him now, gentle

hands running over his torso, then moving to his back and his injury. He hissed as she touched the cut. "I can't believe my toxin didn't work on him."

"Here." Yael shoved something at her. "Put this on the wound."

She ripped open the small packet of powder, then poured the contents onto his back. His whole body clenched with a brief burst of agony, before a blessed numbness spread throughout. Then Yael was there, binding the wound and muttering a few incantations over it.

Dru helped Azrael stand, and then the three of them took in the scene. Two dead horned demons and a decapitated god.

"Why do I get the feeling this isn't over?" Azrael asked.

"It's over. He was over-confident," Yael replied.

Dru didn't look convinced, but whipped her phone out and snapped a photo of the dead sorcerer and his buddies.

"What are you doing?" Yael grabbed her wrist.

Azrael growled low in his throat. *No one* touched Dru.

"Evidence." Her eyes turned inky black, malice seeping through every pore of her body. "If you don't take your hand off me in the next three seconds, I'll claw you up."

Yael's grip visibly tightened before he released her and stepped away, out of range.

She kept her glare on him, then shook her head, her gaze clearing. She slung off her pack and pulled out a velvet bag.

"What's that for?" Yael asked.

"Goodies."

"Goodies?"

"Before I came here, I heard Set had a treasure trove. I am going to collect some things to take back, since you got the kill. I need to give *something* to my guild."

Guilt seared through Azrael. They'd just cost her an opportunity to free herself from blood-slavery.

But if not for Yael, they both might have been dead.

Which is kind of embarrassing. Two seasoned assassins almost being killed by a former god with *just* a sword.

And he knew that Yael would never let him live it down.

"We don't have a lot of time," Dru said, opening the bag.

"Why not?" Yael asked.

"I doubt these were Set's only retainers. And there's that dragon to consider. You guys can stay here if you want, but I am going looting." She walked over to the nearest cabinet, paused, then came back. She crouched by Set's corpse and drew a knife.

"What are you doing?" Azrael asked.

"The cabinets are booby trapped, but I am sure Set's fingerprints or blood will unseal them for us." She lifted the god's limp hand and calmly sliced off two fingers. She held one out to him.

He took it. It was still warm.

Then she was back at the cabinets, muttering to herself.

"We need to find the Orb." Yael's voice was barely above a whisper.

Azrael nodded. "I know."

"Let's go."

The three of them combed through the cabinets in the throne room, Dru pocketing items here and there. Her plan obviously worked.

"It's not here," Yael muttered.

"I think we should go back to the treasure chamber," Azrael said to Dru.

She looked up while she shoved what looked like a crown into the velvet bag, which now bulged with items. "Okay. I want to grab that scepter I saw last time."

He frowned. "The glowing red one?"

"Yeah."

They started walking.

"I told you it was dangerous."

"I still want it."

Story of my life, he thought, staring at her profile.

The journey back through the golden hallway took mere seconds. At the doors to the treasure chamber, Azrael asked, "What do we do about the dragon?"

Dru winced. "Try and avoid it."

Then she was gone through the doors.

Yael raised an eyebrow at her quick departure, then followed her.

Azrael took a deep breath. He hoped that they'd be lucky and find the Orb in here, otherwise they were screwed. It could be anywhere in the castle, and once the retainers realized Set was dead, it was going to be chaos.

He jogged down row after row of artifacts, alert for anything that was remotely spherical. He could see Dru out the corner of his eye, her white head bent over a display case and shoving something glowing into her bag.

He shuddered. That scepter was bad magic.

Wait.

There.

A glowing red-gold orb hung suspended within a display case. Light pulsed from it in a steady wave, strong as a heartbeat. Azrael stared down at the small label, the words written in an elegant cursive script: *'Odin's Orb.'*

There was more text below it, but there was no time to read it now. He'd take it with him.

Pressing the severed finger to the gold panel at the front of the case, he clenched his teeth and waited for a spell to blast out. Nothing happened except a faint clicking sound. He let out a long breath as the front glass pane swung open, and there was the Orb.

He grabbed it, hissing at the intense coldness that burned his fingers on contact, then shoved it and the note into a side pocket of his pack.

"Did you find it?" Dru asked.

He jumped a little, turning toward her. "Yeah."

She gave him a sad smile. "Good."

Yael backed into their line of vision, his hands up in a placating gesture. "Ah, guys…"

"What?" Azrael asked.

Then he looked up.

Overhead loomed an arrow-shaped serpentine head, easily big enough to swallow a man whole. Its gold-green scales shimmered in the glimmering light of the treasure chamber as it delicately sniffed the air. Then its red eyes locked on Dru and her bulging bag of loot.

A roar echoed through the room as the dragon reared its head even higher, drawing in a great gust of air.

"*Run!*"

They darted through the maze of cabinets, heading for the exit. A blast of hot air singed their backs as the dragon exhaled a mouthful of flames, and a hot wind battered them as the beast took to the air.

Azrael's breath sawed through his lungs as darted spells and cases. *Now I know why the ceiling is so high.*

Dru stopped suddenly, and Azrael barely avoided body-slamming her to the ground. She was standing under a case with a little overhang, there to provide additional to shelter the object within. The velvet sack was shoved awkwardly under her one arm. "Grab my hand!"

He immediately latched on, watching as Yael ceased running. "What are you doing?"

"Come here!"

"We have to leave, now!"

"Come here!"

For a split second, it looked as if Yael would leave them for dead, but he sprinted back, latching onto Dru's arm.

That's when Azreal saw the green glow.

Dru spun the ring on her finger quickly, just as a fiery blast shot down from above. The heat was so intense Azrael's skin began to blister, the hairs on his arms crisping.

We're going to die.

CHAPTER 29

Dru gasped a mouthful of fresh air as her knees gave out and she collapsed onto her butt. Az and Yael were on their hands and knees, panting over the immaculate lawn.

That had been close.

Way too close.

"We made it," Dru said, then started coughing. Her throat had been burned in those final seconds, while she had struggled to concentrate on a way out of the dragon's path. But she'd managed to focus enough so the ring could do its job.

She was convinced now that Hermes' little gemstone reacted to danger, because there didn't seem to be any regular interval when it came to recharging. Maybe danger and lust, since the ring had been meant for one of his lovers.

I'll guess I'll find out. It wasn't like the ring was going anywhere, after all.

"Couldn't you have teleported us out *earlier*?" Yael demanded, his head snapping up, disdain stamped on his face.

He was handsome, she supposed. The shiny brown hair, olive skin and hazel eyes were a striking mix with his chiseled features. But there was something about the guy that irritated her—like a sibling she'd prefer not to have to visit too often. Oh, and he was an arrogant asshole.

"Not how the ring works," she replied.

The skin on her left arm was blistered, but it'd heal soon enough. She peeled her shirt away from the wounds, hissing as her fried nerve-endings came back to life in a storm of activity.

Dragon fire.

Damn, they were lucky to be alive.

Even angels could be incinerated by a blaze that intense.

Slowly, she pushed herself to her feet, taking in their new location: the Human Realm. Not a hint of sulfur in the air, just woodsmoke, chemical fumes, and an open blue sky lit by a fierce sun. The glossy dark-green grass she'd landed on was dissected by a pebbled pathway that led toward a series of elaborate gardens. Behind them soared the ornate columned entryway of Az's mansion, and a Devilsgate swirled merrily near their front door.

It's still there.

Huh. She'd thought it had been summoned just for the party. Maybe they had one here all the time.

They are seriously rich.

"You brought us home?" Az asked. He'd come quietly to his feet and edged next to her. She wanted to lean against him, to feel his heartbeat against her cheek, to reassure herself that he was fine after being stabbed and then burned, but Yael was watching them with a hawk-like gleam in his eyes.

"Seemed like the best place." She hadn't tried the guild again, not wanting to bring two angels into their headquarters. The fall-out—for *her*—wouldn't have been pretty. Sure, she might have been able to sneak Az in for a few hours, but she had the feeling that Yael would cause trouble, just because he could.

"Thank you." Az's voice was quiet, but she heard the wealth of meaning in those two words.

She shouldn't drag this out. She had to go. Had to return to her shitty normal life, and try to bargain for freedom for her and her sister. If Trick was holding Az's buddy captive, then the entire guild was at risk; no matter how awkward her relationship with Peony, she wasn't going to leave her sister to become fodder for an angel rampage.

Which would no doubt happen as soon as Az and his buddies found out about the hidden angel—even if he wasn't their friend. Despite the fact that Az had been booted from Heaven on a flimsy excuse, his loyalty would no doubt be to others of his kind first; cambions like her, second.

"We had a deal," Dru murmured.

Az's expression turned bleak. "Will I see you again?"

She didn't want to lie to him, so she said, "Maybe." Even though she had no intention of bumping into him again—ever—she couldn't predict the future.

She reached out and gave him a quick hug, her hands sliding up his back. As she stepped away from the embrace, she adjusted her pack and bent down to pick up the storage bag she'd dropped earlier. It had been definitely worth the cost—a Mary Poppins-style sack that was bigger on the inside than the outside. She had so much loot crammed in there she would have slipped a disc in her spine if she'd had to lug around the real weight.

"Aww, aren't you two cute?" Sarcasm oozed from Yael's words. "Az, stop trying to fuck the demon and get inside." Then the brown-haired angel turned to her. "Let's hope I never see you again."

She met his stare, her inner monster rising to the surface. "Likewise."

Az pressed his lips together, but didn't say anything.

"Does that Devilsgate still take you wherever you want to go?" she asked.

Az looked at Yael, who had been joined by two others at the entrance to the mansion. The beautiful ebony-skinned woman glared at Dru like she was a cockroach that needed stomping, while the other dark-skinned angel's expression was unreadable. They were all inhumanly beautiful—and wingless.

So, they'd all paid the same price.

The woman nodded. "Yes, it does."

"Then thanks. It's been a blast." She winked at Az and sauntered over to the portal. *Don't look back*, she told herself. She didn't owe Az anything, and well, she could try and help him indirectly when she was free. But until the invisible bonds of slavery vanished, she didn't have a lot of options left to her.

She had to get free.

Taking a deep breath, she stepped through the Devilsgate and back into the Halcyon Guild.

Bye, Az.

✖

The guild was in mild chaos when she arrived. Assassins and other personnel were running all over the place, heads down and in so much of a hurry three of them nearly collided with her. The few colleagues who actually met her stare all turned their gaze away quickly, as if to avoid snagging her attention.

Sure, she wasn't the most liked assassin out there, but she usually warranted more than a grunt, even from Metcalf, the guild's Reynard's Imp.

Striding into the main hall, she spotted Trick lounging on his 'throne' at the end of the room. She'd always thought it an impressive chair, but now she'd seen Set's castle. His throne shat all over Trick's in style, wealth, and sheer decorative value.

Trick came to his feet quickly, looking a little wild-eyed.

Something was wrong.

She paused halfway up the room, then pressed on. Had something happened to Peony? *I shouldn't have been so self-centered. I should have said something to Trick about the angel...*

The fact that her boss was looking uncertain, and that no one would meet her gaze—

Peony better not be dead.

Hell would rain down if she was.

Trick lowered himself back to his throne, but he still didn't look quite right. His normal cloak of arrogance was gone, replaced with false cheer. "You're back!"

"It took a little longer than I thought, but it's done."

Both of his golden eyebrows rose. "Set is dead?"

She showed him the picture on her phone—the black blood and headless body.

Trick went to speak, but she cut him off with a slash of her hand. "What's going on?"

"Uhh, nothing."

She stared at him, something dark welling to the surface. He was lying to her. "Where is Peony?"

"Uhh, we can talk about that later."

She set her stance, leaning forward a little, her earlier guilt burning a hole in her chest. "No, we can't."

Something in her expression must have shown how close to the edge she was, because Trick shoved a hand through his hair, then heaved out a deep sigh.

"Some Mortus demons came here, looking for a half-Mortus cambion with white hair and golden skin—"

Shock rooted her to the spot, before rage unlike anything she'd experience before ripped through her, reducing her human veneer to ash. "You *didn't*."

Trick gave a helpless shrug. "They weren't going to leave. And they're powerful."

"You sold Peony to the Mortus?" She was shouting, but she didn't care. Stepping forward, she grabbed Trick by the shirtfront and hauled him to his feet, her strength fueled by the dark monster inside that had erupted from its restraints. "Do you understand what they are like? What they will *do* to her?"

"I wasn't going to wait to give them *you*." His brown eyes turned cold. No, Peony wasn't as useful as a hired killer.

He kept talking, "I'll give you some slack because your sister is gone, but touch me again like that, and things won't turn out nicely. I am still your boss."

Not for fucking long.

He stepped back.

"I didn't do the kill," she said, slowly.

Trick settled back onto his throne. "Then you failed."

"Yes. But I got all this." She opened the Mary Poppins bag, light spilling out, highlighting the treasures within.

Trick snapped a finger at Errant, a hovering demon. "Excellent. Take it to the treasury."

"I don't think so."

"Excuse me?"

"I was only sent to kill Set and retrieve a certain artifact. I did not kill Set, and the artifact is not in my stash. Therefore, this is not guild property. It is *mine*."

Anger flared briefly to life in her boss' eyes, but considering they were being watched by other milling guild members, he couldn't force her to give up the goods. It was one of the guild's rules—do the job, and any other benefits were yours to pocket. Unless you were tricked out of them.

Errant, the guild's administration officer and financier, moved forward, looking into the sack. He gave a low whistle. "There's a king's ransom of magical artifacts here."

Trick glared at him and the demon scuttled away.

"This is enough to buy my freedom twice over," Dru said, dropping the bag onto the floor with a thud.

"You want to leave." Trick's voice was flat. "Look, with that, you could put it toward buying Peony back from the Mortus—"

"They won't give her up. You know that, as do I."

"You've never had anything to do with them."

"Not true."

His eyes narrowed.

"It's no coincidence they came looking for someone of *my* description. And you sold them the wrong demon. Nice." She kicked the bag then turned to Errant. "Take that and settle my debt. Credit me whatever is left over."

She hadn't been sure there'd be enough to buy freedom for her *and* Peony, but that didn't matter anymore, did it?

"Think about it, Dru. You haven't got any friends outside the guild. Buying your freedom will get you nothing."

"It will get me out of here."

Her anger was brighter, hotter than she thought she could control. But she remembered how Az had been betrayed, how he had fought through the agony of deceit and was trying to reclaim his life.

She could do nothing less.

Except Trick had *stolen* from her.

Oh, she'd never trusted him, but she'd thought she could rely on him.

More fool me.

Well, she wasn't above screwing someone over in return.

As she went to leave, Trick's voice stopped her. "What about the Orb? Do you know where it is?"

Dru swiveled on her heel, facing her soon-to-be-former master. "I know where it is."

"And?"

"An angel beat me to retrieving it."

Then she walked out the hall, and into her new life.

CHAPTER 30

"Fuck!"

Az searched his backpack for a second time, but all he had was the note. Every piece of his gear was spread out across the huge glass table in their dining room, and there was no magical artifact among them. Yael, Raze and Seraphina were watching him with wary stares.

Dru.

She'd given him that quick hug before she disappeared through the gate—her hands had slid up his back and…

"Motherfucker!"

She'd stolen the Orb from him.

She'd known how important it was, and she'd *still* taken it. He'd been played for a fool the entire time. And the worst part? He'd wanted to see her again. Not just for the sex—which had been amazing—but because she'd managed to steal a bit of his heart. He'd thought they could have had a future together. Even if it meant he'd never get his wings back for loving a cambion, he would have taken the risk.

You're a complete idiot, being led around by your cock.

"What's wrong?" Seraphina's smooth voice interrupted his pity-party.

"It's gone."

"What's gone?"

"The Orb."

"You let her take it?" Yael's voice was like a whip.

Azrael's head snapped up. "Yeah, I just handed it to her. Asshole."

The brown-haired angel held up his hands. "I just...you had it and you lost it."

"Thanks for having my back. I didn't see you finding the thing."

"Enough!" Raze barked. "We will just get it back."

"That might not be so easy," he admitted. "She works for the Halcyon Guild."

"They were here the other night." Seraphina sniffed, disdain in her brown eyes. "Their leader, Trick, tried to make pretty with us. He was probably planning on double-crossing us the entire time."

"Why would he want the Orb, though?" Raze asked.

"Why does anyone?" she countered.

"Power?" Az asked.

"Because it can show you anything you want to see—and can tell you how to get it," Raze said quietly.

Silence descended for a few heartbeats.

Funny how Azrael had gone haring off after the thing, and he hadn't really cared about what it could do. It showed how much he'd changed since losing his wings. He'd never done anything without fully knowing what he was stepping into; had always been cautious and deliberate about achieving his goals.

"Set had it for centuries, but he never seemed to use it," Azrael said, breaking the quiet.

Raze picked up the label—all that Az had of the Orb—and read it. He flipped it over, then cursed.

"What?"

He handed the gilded paper to Az. The front read, *'Odin's Orb—A mystical portal into the past, present and future'*.

"Look at the back," Raze said, his voice somber.

Azrael read the reverse. *'Can only be used by a demon who is "pure of heart".'* His fingers went slack. No wonder Set had never taken advantage of the weapon. He couldn't use it.

No one could.

Azrael sat slumped in an armchair in his chambers, a glass of whiskey in one hand. It was an expensive brand, straight from Raze's own personal collection, but it tasted like ashes to him. He'd been betrayed not once, but twice.

First Heaven.

Now Dru.

And both times over something that was completely unobtainable: Heaven's Heart—find all three missing pieces; and Odin's Orb—could only be used by a demon who is pure of heart. He gave a mirthless chuckle and took another sip.

Yael had wanted to rail at him some more for losing the Orb, but Raze had stopped him. What was the point, when they couldn't use it, anyway?

He just wanted to direct his anger somewhere.

And Azrael was an easy enough target, he supposed.

"Hello, Azrael."

He jolted in his seat, slopping expensive Scotch onto the expensive rug. An angel had appeared in the room, gold-threaded wings arched behind her gracefully, tucked in neatly behind her back. She wore a gown so tight it might have been painted on, the generous swell of her breasts and a perfectly toned thigh exposed by its cut, and she favored him with an amused look.

"Aurora," he said, shocked.

"You know who I am?" Had she batted her eyelashes? Her gaze roamed over his body, coming to rest at his bare feet.

"Every angel knows who the archangels are." Because Aurora was one of the fourteen archangels who ruled Heaven. She hadn't been there the day Uriel had sliced the wings from Azrael's back; he'd only been worthy of three archangels to witness his disgrace, Michael, Uriel and Gabriel.

The enforcers.

"How can I help you?" he asked. Because she wasn't here for a social visit. Not one of the Darts had earned the pleasure of an angelic presence since they'd fallen.

"I'd like to offer you a position." Her voice was like honeyed sugar. Despite his ability to tell truth from lie, he didn't trust it one bit.

"Doing what, exactly?"

She smiled kindly at him. "I am in need of a Consort—one who can help me."

He waited for something to stir within: a sense of pride that she'd come to him; excitement at the idea of being with an *archangel*. But he felt hollow. And suspicious. Why had she suddenly decided *now* to come up with the offer? Not the decades previously when he'd been a dedicated soldier with a perfect record?

"I am flattered, if you are implying that *I* am a candidate for such an illustrious role."

Her mouth pressed to a thin line when he said nothing more. "You would be a serious contender, if you could help me find something." She ran her hands over her torso, lingering on her generous hips.

But her luscious body didn't do anything for him. In fact, his cock couldn't be any less interested.

She was a viper. She wanted to use him as a pet assassin, someone to do her dirty work. The consort bit had just been tacked on to lure him to her side, like a moth to a flame. Too bad he'd already been burned.

Literally and figuratively.

But telling her he wasn't interested probably wasn't a clever idea. "What do you need found?"

"Odin's Orb."

He stared at her, and laughter threatened to escape from his chest. They wanted the Orb. That meant, if it could be used, it was powerful enough to warrant even archangel attention. "It's long gone."

Aurora approached him and ran a gentle finger down his cheek. The overpowering scent of lilies jarred through him, and he resisted the impulse to jerk away. "I am sure you can find it again," she breathed.

"It's with a demon who has no intention of giving it back. Trust me on that."

"But couldn't you try? For me?" she purred.

"No."

She reared away at his refusal, her gaze wide with

incredulity. "No?"

"I am not going to chase down the Orb in a den full of assassins. It is being held in one of the most powerful demon assassination guilds in all three circles of Hell."

All of which was true.

But the real reason? He didn't want to see Dru again, didn't want to hear her excuses. Because he knew she had them, and he knew they were probably damned good ones.

"But you're an angel warrior."

"I *was* one." He let some of his rage at how the Darts had been treated shine through in his expression. "If you reinstate my wings—and those of my friends—then we'd be easily powerful enough to retrieve the Orb."

Her features turned cold. "That is not a decision I can make on my own. And you know there is only one way to earn your wings back."

"Then I am very sorry, but I must decline your generous offer. However, if you ever think of a different task that might be achievable..." He let his sentence hang.

She stretched her wings out behind her, their tips almost spanning the width of his room. "There won't ever be a second offer."

Then she was gone.

And he was alone, back where he'd started.

Screwed.

CHAPTER 31

I am an idiot.

Yeah, she totally was. But Trick had fucked her over, big time. He'd sold her sister to the damned Mortus demons. *Peony!* To the *Mortus*.

Dru wasn't going to let her sister rot in the hands of those scumbags...but she was going to need help getting her back.

She waited for a few seconds, holding her breath as Sylvester wandered down the hallway to her left. He was another cambion, rare and expensive—a Pollus/human mix. It meant he had some basic healing abilities, but he was more interested in killing and stealing than helping others. Said he took after his human side.

The demon was wearing fighting leathers, and pulling latex gloves off his hands as he walked. Now that Peony was gone, the guild didn't really have a medic, so he was helping out.

That poor angel. Sylvester wasn't really known for his bedside manner.

After the cambion vanished from sight, Dru hurried in

the direction he'd just come from, tugging her backpack strap higher up on her shoulder. Everything she owned was in the pack, including the papers that proclaimed she was free.

Free.

But still trapped.

Within moments, she was at the door of a cell. It had taken her three days of trailing Sylvester and avoiding Trick to find the entrance to this hidden prison. Her ex-boss really wasn't taking any chances.

You can't go back if you do this.

No.

But she couldn't go forward, either.

Taking a deep breath, she gripped the door handle and swung the heavy metal portal open.

The angel lay on the floor, his wings a gnarled mess of baby feathers and exposed bone and sinew. *Gross.* Wisps of blond hair covered a head that had recently been shaved, and he was face-down on the ground.

At the sound of her footsteps, he lifted his head, his eyes widening at her presence. A sizzle of awareness passed between them, and he looked at her like a starving man might eye a banquet. But then his expression changed to bewilderment.

"You aren't...*her*."

He'd definitely met Peony before. And he could tell the difference between them, even at a glance. Dru filed his initial reaction away to ponder later.

"No, I'm her sister."

His head dropped. "She's gone."

"Want to help me get her back?" Dru asked, leaning against the door frame like she had all the time in the world. Inside, though, her heart was pounding with worry. She had no idea when Trick or Sylvester might come by to check on the prisoner.

A bitter chuckle rose in the air. "What am I going to be able to do?"

"Well, you are an angel. And you aren't fallen."

Green eyes blazed up at her. "I may as well be."

"You have wings."

He snorted.

"They look like they're growing back. And I might know a guy who can help you."

Hope flared in his emerald stare. "What are you saying?"

"Come with me."

"And go where?"

That was a good question. And considering she was probably stealing one of Trick's newest blood-slaves...

"To a friend's."

"I'm not really in any condition to walk."

"First," Dru said, squatting next to him. "We make a deal."

Bitterness and resentment crept into his face. "Like what?"

"You have to help me find Peony when you're well."

His eyes widened. "Deal."

A tingle spread out along her spine as the magic of the promise took hold. "Then let's go."

CHAPTER 32

Uriel glanced up as Aurora slammed into his sitting room. "How did it go?"

"Terribly." She sat down on the chair across from him, her golden eyes flashing. A bare second later, Gabriel and Michael appeared. The power of three other archangels pulsed against Uriel's skin, the urge to strike out at them mild. That was the problem with archangels—there was always an underlying competitiveness between them.

Aurora flicked her long mane of honey-gold hair over her shoulder. She was beautiful—one of the most stunning creatures to ever grace the Heavens—but she left Uriel cold. The heart of a snake lived within her breast, something he could relate to, even admire. "He said he wouldn't look for the Orb," she said.

"He didn't have it?" Michael asked.

"He said he didn't, and he wasn't lying. It was stolen from him after he took it from Set."

"Then why did he not offer to find it?"

"He said it was too dangerous. That he would only do it if his wings were restored."

The comment left a stunned silence in its wake.

"He *refused* a request from an archangel?"

She nodded, her face tight.

"I assume you didn't offer him his wings back," Gabriel said, his deep voice thundering.

Her eyes flashed. "I am not a fool."

"Then you clearly didn't offer him a good enough incentive," Michael commented.

"Look at her. She offered him more than a pat on the head," Uriel said silkily.

"They don't have the Orb. So they can't use it. We didn't really lose," she said, although the look on her face threatened revenge on the upstart Azrael.

To think, a former warrior-class angel refusing an archangel's request. It wasn't to be borne. Then again, technically those wingless fools didn't answer to Heaven anymore, so they *could* refuse. But it was going to be remembered, if they ever won the Heart back.

Which would never happen.

"Any report on Set?" Michael asked.

Set had been a thorn in their sides for eons, as had his brother, Osiris. It was too bad that both were largely out of reach.

"He was dismembered by one of the angels. But considering the curse on him and his brother...unless a primordial god of the dead touches his body, he will regenerate."

And primordial gods were few and far between after the Culling. They'd ensured it.

"A pity."

CHAPTER 33

Azrael hurried through the foyer; someone was banging persistently on the front door.

Raze and Seraphina were out scoping other leads, but their disappointment was still thick in the air. He'd failed them, not just once, but twice. Yael and Seraphina hadn't been happy about his refusal to placate Aurora, but Raze had sided with him. A secretive man by nature, Raze was a born skeptic, and he, too, doubted the supposed good fortune of Aurora's 'interest'.

He was about three yards from the door when Yael appeared, jerking the portal open. The angel's back went ramrod straight, then he lunged out at whoever was on the threshold.

"Touch me and I'll cut you a new fucking smile!"

No.

She wouldn't have come back—

"Motherfucker!" shouted Yael, and Azrael sprinted through the door.

Dru had the angel pinned to the mosaic-tiled ground, her claws unsheathed. Azrael flung himself at her, arms looping around her waist, and he rolled away from Yael with her.

But as he did so, Yael stabbed upward, knife sinking into his side.

"*Yael!*"

"Shit!"

They toppled down the stairs, coming to a jarring halt on the driveway. Azrael lay on his back, Dru next to him. He grabbed the handle of the knife then plucked it free. "Why do I always get stabbed when you're around?"

Panicked gray eyes met his, and her hands pressed against his wound. "Are you okay?"

"I will be." He dropped the dagger on the ground.

Yael hovered over them, frowning, and picked up the knife. "What did you do to the blade?"

Azrael frowned. "Nothing."

"It's like acid has eaten it away."

Next to him, Dru spoke up. "Can I see it?"

"I can shove it in your—"

"*Yael.*"

"Fine." He handed her the blade. As it passed over Azrael's head, he spotted the pits and pockmarks on the dull metal.

Dru studied the blade in silence then handed it back.

Yael glared at her. "Do you know what the deal is?"

"I might have an idea."

"Care to share?"

"Not right now, no."

"Look—"

"I have another couple of pressing matters you might be interested in," Dru said, cutting him off.

Azrael sat up, coughing a little at the pain, but it was

already beginning to recede. "What trouble did you bring with you?"

"Why do you assume it's trouble?" she grumbled.

Azrael raised an eyebrow.

Dru sighed. "Wait here."

She disappeared across the grass, and vanished behind a manicured shrub.

"What do you think she's doing?" Azrael wondered.

"I can't believe she had the gall to show up here," Yael said, glaring at him. "You should have let me stab her."

Dru reappeared, hefting something upright. "You might want to take the back."

Azrael sprinted toward her, clutching at his side, which was already healing. He was half-convinced he was seeing an illusion. A battered face, torn and shredded wings, and eyes so green they reminded him of the gardens in Heaven.

"*Zadkiel*?"

A bob of the head in reply.

Azrael quickly draped the man's free arm over his shoulder, and then he and Dru walked the injured angel up the stairs and into the foyer. Yael followed hot on their heels, his phone out as he called Raze or Seraphina, as well as sending out a mental blast that nearly deafened Azrael's mind.

They carefully laid Zadkiel on a backless sofa, the injured angel grunting with the effort. It hurt Azrael to look at his emaciated wings, the pin feathers and exposed sinew. The torture he would have had to go through to end up with such an injury…

Azrael looked over Zadkiel's prone body at Dru, who stood off to the side. "Where did you find him?"

"My guild had him."

Azrael snapped to his full height. "What? You knew the whole time—?" Another sweeping lash of betrayal stung him.

"I had heard we had an angel captured, but I didn't know he was your friend. I still had no idea when I removed him from the guild." Truth.

He shut his eyes briefly.

"But you brought him here anyway."

Her expression was serious. "It was the only safe place I could think of for an angel."

"You stole the Orb," Yael accused.

Dru turned to him, her eyes bleeding black. "It was part of my mission. And it was going to buy freedom for my sister and me."

He noticed she said *was*.

I knew she was going to have a reason.

But did it make him feel any different?

"Freedom?" Yael asked.

"I was a blood-slave. So is my sister."

"What happened to her?" Azrael asked, moving closer to Dru, her strength alluring, drawing him in. Could he ever get enough of her? Even with everything that had happened between them?

Her eyes seemed to swallow all the light, their inky darkness all-consuming. "Trick sold her to the Mortus."

Surprise shot through him.

"He betrayed me."

"You betrayed us," Yael snapped.

Azrael wanted to deny that, but it was true.

Dru nodded, the black receding from her eyes. "I did. But only for our freedom. I would have tried to help after."

Truth.

From the shock in Yael's eyes, he too heard the sincerity in the words.

She hadn't truly screwed Azrael over. Sure, she'd stolen the Orb, and he may never have gotten it back, but she'd planned on helping him later. That *did* count for something, at least for him.

"And, well...here." Dru reached into her pack and pulled out a cloth-wrapped bundle. She shoved it at him.

He grabbed it automatically, and his eyes widened at the feel of it in his palm. He unwrapped the package, exposing a red-golden ball that glowed with an inner fire.

"Is that—?" Yael whispered.

"It's the Orb."

"You didn't hand it over to Trick?" Azrael asked.

She shook her head.

Hurried footsteps sounded in the hall and then Raze and Seraphina were in the room, their shouts and cries distracting from the Orb. Both hurried to Zadkiel, running gentle hands over the skin of the angel's back, careful to avoid his ruined wings, talking to him softly.

Eventually, Raze's eyes settled on the glowing sphere in Azrael's hand, before swinging back to Dru.

"She brought you the Orb?" the dark-skinned angel asked.

"And Zadkiel."

His storm-cloud-colored eyes darkened. "Thank you. But why?"

"My sister was sold to the Mortus. She was caring for your buddy, helping him heal. I made a deal with him. He's going to help me get her back." She nodded at

Azrael. "And I thought I should return the Orb to you. You need it more than I do."

Fuck. He felt another piece of his heart break away, forever stolen by Dru.

"Thank you," he said, staring at her, the others in the room receding.

"That's lovely and all," Yael cut in. "But we can't use it."

"No one can," Seraphina said.

"*What*?" Dru's voice was a whip.

"Only a demon who is 'pure of heart' can use the Orb," Azrael explained.

Dru and Zadkiel locked gazes, then the angel spoke softly. "The little healer."

Dru nodded. "My sister."

Yael laughed. "There is no such thing as a demon who is 'pure of heart'."

"Peony was raised by humans," Dru said. "She went to medical school, intending to become a doctor. She just wants to help people."

"She is kind. Pure." Zadkiel struggled to rise. "We must save her."

Seraphina pushed him back down with gentle hands. "You must heal first."

Azrael handed the Orb to Raze, then grabbed Dru's arm, pulling her across the room. Fuck, she was the best thing he'd seen all day. All year. His whole life.

"Are you sure?" he asked.

"About Peony? Yes. She is *good*, Az, not like me." Her expression was earnest.

"No, about coming here."

"I had nowhere else to go. I am sorry about stealing

the Orb, but I really did think it was the only way to free us."

He raised his hands to cup her cheeks. She leaned into the touch. "I forgive you."

She let out a strangled sound, a mix of a sob and laugh. "You're an angel, you have to."

"No, I don't."

Then he leaned down, kissing her, tasting salt on her lips.

It was like coming home.

Dru pulled away first, her gray eyes searching his. "I just want you to know that I think I kind of love you. Just a bit." She held her fingers an inch apart.

Truth.

He could guess how much that admission had cost her, because he knew what it was going to cost him. "That's okay, I feel the same." He stroked a thumb over her cheek.

She wrapped her arms around his waist, pressing her cheek to his chest. "That's good, because I think you're my mate."

His hands froze on her arms. "*What*?"

"Your blood turning to acid. It's not always a side-effect, but you absorbed my toxin and now you can't sleep with anyone but me, not without causing them some problems." She mumbled most of that against his shirt.

"So now *my* man parts are toxic?" He laughed. He couldn't have taken Aurora up on her offer, even if he had wanted to.

A hesitant smile. "Are you angry?"

He shook his head, resting his chin on her head. He

inhaled deeply, the scent of jasmine clinging to her. "Aren't we a pair?"

"So what now?" she asked.

He pretended to think about it. "I reckon you move in, we have lots of sex, and we find your sister."

"Sounds good to me."

He raised his eyebrows, expression wicked. "Want to make it a deal?"

A low chuckle. "Deal."

The tingle of magic rushed through him, and then he was kissing her like she was the only woman in the universe, and she was kissing him back like he was vital to her survival.

"Whoa guys, *gross*." Yael's voice cut into their passion.

Azrael lifted his head, glaring at his friend. "Fuck off."

"Can I stab him, just a little bit?" Dru asked, half-turning in his embrace.

"Later."

Then he swept her off her feet and carried her to his room.

He had a bargain to fulfil.

ACKNOWLEDGMENTS

No book is created in a vacuum—we're inspired by many strange and wonderful things. In this instance, *Deadly Passion* was brought to life by a conversation I had with fellow author, Kel Carpenter. So Kel, thank you! I'd also like to thank my husband Tom, my wonderful beta reader Joanne Danton, and my eagle-eyed editor Pete Kempshall. All your thoughts and comments—even the painful ones!—made this book better.

Amanda Pillar is an USA Today Bestselling author and award-winning editor, who lives in Australia. She's the author of the unique Graced series, the PNR adventure series, Heaven's Heart, and the standalone, *Haunt Me*.

She has had over a dozen short stories published and has edited nine anthologies over the years. People say it's because she's an 'over-achiever' but, in reality, Amanda doesn't understand the concept of 'relaxation'. (Please feel free to explain it to her. Use small words.) Compounding this issue, Amanda also designs book covers and has commenced work on a PhD. Because she's crazy.

Oh, and in her day job, she's an archaeologist.

For more information please visit:

http://www.amandapillar.com